Black woman in the nigh

Black woman in the night sky is a collection of forty poems, most dealing with contemporary social issues, such as racism, anti-semitism, the treatment of refugees, violence, sexual harassment, infidelity, prostitution, megalomania, the working environment, unemployment, eugenics, euthanasia, the failure of community, and the collapse of communism.

The web of meaning is woven from the bright weft of the language of ordinary people and the dark warp of ideas from philosophers and social commentators, such as Hegel, Marx, Nietzsche, Heidegger and Sartre. Despite an urban subject-matter, deliberately selected, and sometimes presented in sordid and shocking ways, these poignant poems possess an inner serenity and disciplined spiritual detachment that promise humankind a fundamentally optimistic future.

Frank Reeves writes in what has been dubbed a counter-romantic style, owing much to nineteenth-century British poets, in particular, Shelley, Tennyson, Arnold, Browning, and Hardy, but spurning heroic theme and pastoral metaphor in favour of the post-industrial white-collar office and urban world. Frank was born in Birmingham, is resident in Wolverhampton, and has been engaged for most of his life in the politics of race relations. He has dedicated his book to his mentor, Niranjan Singh Noor, the great Panjabi poet and activist, who died suddenly in 1999 from an asthma attack.

The Progressive Writers' Association (GB), in association with the Education Now Publishing Co-operative, has produced a book of exquisite poetry that helps us to examine afresh our alienated urban relationships. Here is an opportunity to enjoy an exciting, but often appalling, poetic insight into the mundane world of the computer, traffic jam, back garden, or office block.

BLACK WOMAN
IN THE NIGHT SKY

Multi-cultural, anti-racist
and progressive verse

by Frank Reeves

**Progressive Writers' Association (GB)
in association with
Education Now Publishing Co-operative**

First published in Great Britain in 2000 by the Progressive Writers'
Association in association with Education Now Publishing Co-operative Ltd,
PO Box 186, Derby, England. This book has been wholly produced by an
independent member of the Education Now Publishing Co-operative and
written for a purpose other than the direct promotion of the aims and
objectives of Education Now, but details about the work of Education Now is
included herein.

British Cataloguing in Publication Data

Black Woman in the Night Sky
1 Poetry 2 Multi-cultural 3 Progressive Writers
I Title
III Reeves, Frank W.

ISBN 1 871526 48 5

Printed by Esparto Digital Ltd, England
Price £6.00

**This book is dedicated to my friend,
Niranjan Singh Noor,
and to the authors of the
Progressive Writers' Association (GB)**

The pen became your *kirpan* sword
As, dressed in the fine *kach* breeches
Of education, you rode out
To the war of the classes on
A white charger of poetry.

Acknowledgements

The author wishes to acknowledge:

The poet, Niranjan Singh Noor, since deceased, for encouraging him to improve and publish his verse.

The writer and president of the Progressive Writers' Association (G B), Darshan Singh Dhir, for his support, encouragement, and ready agreement to promote and publish these poems.

The novelist, poet, critic and scholar, Dr Swaran Chandan, for his willingness to read the poems and to write such an erudite introduction.

The poet, Dr Davinder Chandan, for her friendship, encouragement and for introducing him to her husband, Swaran.

His academic collaborator and confidante, Dr Anna Frankel, for sharing her knowledge of literature, for her helpful comments on early drafts, and for her insightful preface.

His former tutor and business associate, Professor Roland Meighan, and Education Now, for advising and assisting with publishing and marketing.

His former secretaries, Perminder Bains and Shirley McFarquhar, for their help in processing the manuscript.

His wife, Professor Mel Chevannes, for poetic inspiration, but especially for tolerating both his malingering as a writer and the disruptive displacement to domestic life caused by his obsessive behaviour.

His children, Toussaint, Spartaca and Robeson, for penetrating comments on early drafts.

His children's former nanny and family friend, Margaret Potter, for practical support, kindness, and an insistence on simplicity of expression.

His father, Norman Charles, who, even in his nineties, provided advice on linguistic matters and took upon himself the role, rather like a Catholic bishop, of moral censor (all expurgations since restored).

His mother, Phyllis, for inculcating an early affection for poetic language and for showing great enthusiasm for his poem about St Francis.

His friend, Niranjan Singh Dhillon, for his moral support and good humour.

His colleagues, Waqar Azmi, Zahoor Ahmad, Tahir Abbas and Debee Hack, for lively discussions about cultural, moral and religious issues, often resulting in poetic inspiration.

Contents

Preface

by Dr Anna Frankel

I have watched the gestation of this book, following it from its inception through to preparation for publication. At some stage in this process, we engaged in a discussion about theory. How could the poems be situated in literary theory – in relation to other literature? Gradually, the concept of counter-romanticism was born.

The idea of romanticism, in fact, lies along a very long continuum embracing extravagant statements about personal liberation, celebration of the authenticity of the individual (often through expression of non-rule bound action), recognition of the existence of the irrational, and an acknowledgement of the role of the unconscious in human behaviour. In the visible world, romanticism endows features of the natural world with moral significance and, at its most extreme, offers metaphysical interpretations of the historical and political world. Counter-romanticism must, therefore, be seen as the opposite trend: the antithesis of romanticism. But, I suggest, romanticism is such a broad category that it already embraces within itself its own antithesis. What then, in this context, can counter-romanticism be?

From the romantic perspective, Frank Reeves's work is deeply concerned with the moral consequences of action for both himself and others, as illustrated in his poems *I'm a Jew* and *Easter resurrection*. His response to apparently unreflective action is, at least, ambivalent, as well as quietly humorous, as in *Racist Graffiti*. He does not, therefore, celebrate the irrational, the metaphysical, or the unconscious, although he does acknowledge the spiritual dimension, as can be seen in *Anita Garibaldi* and *Night in Assisi*.

In countering romanticism, however, he accepts elements of the modernist thesis by exploring the impoverished and alienated existence of many of his subjects. *Woman Scarecrow*, *Harlech Point* and *Mixed verse: redundancy in the urban forest* are good examples. With one or two exceptions, such as *Lesson in leadership*, he does not portray, as T S Eliot does, the alienation of his characters. On the contrary, he demonstrates a far more Brechtian approach, presenting the facts of social injustice as if they were shockingly unnatural and totally surprising. Read *Ave Maria* and *Sawoniuk of British Rail*, where he does not invite the reader to empathise, but to feel anger and disgust, and, in Maria's case, to acknowledge her as a victim of injustice. How ridiculous, how stupid, we are expected to think.

It is this tendency in Frank Reeves's work that suggests a counter to romanticism: the rejection of metaphysics, irrespective of whether it is articulated in religious belief, as in *Night in Assisi,* or in secular ideology, as in *Technophilia.* Nevertheless, you can only counter what you acknowledge, and Frank always acknowledges the centrality of social forms, structures and systems. Critically, he acknowledges history – his own and that of others – that is a shared history. He is not a post-modernist, although he does make use of symbols and icons deliberately to shock as, for example, in *Community (tribute to Nietzsche).* This technique is one used by post-modernists but, in Frank's work, it is closer to the Brechtian distancing technique, rather than to the methods of the post-modernists, who reject the possibility of resonance associated with the persistence of meaning.

In what further way might these poems be countering romanticism? Do they offer a picture of a natural world without moral significance? If this is so, in what way would this stance be measurably different from that of many other modern poets? For, surely, pure romanticism as represented, say, in the works of Wordsworth or Keats has long been eschewed. Do the verses counter by offering an alternative framework of moral significance in the products of the created, the manufactured world, that human beings have formed? In some cases, such as *Harlech Point* and *The road from Eisingrug,* Frank does indeed appear to accept the post-modern rejection of grand theories of continuing enlightenment.

But thematically, the main focus of his work is on the consequences of oppositional action, as in the poems *Niranjan Singh Noor* and *Geraniums.* The former is optimistic about social action, describing a life that, in rejecting racist ideology and behaviour:

> …bequeathed an armoury
> Of words to your beloved ones:
> Those men and women, black and white,
> Who clamour for equality.

This optimism appears to arise from the apparently unstained banner of anti-racism. In contrast, the central character of *Geraniums,* who has lived his life to bring about the Soviet dream of world communism, is less certain of his epitaph.

One underlying theme is the often-asked question: progress – has it occurred? Are we morally superior to earlier generations? We can see this most vividly in *Antonio Gramsci Avenue, Mermaid murdered at Llandanwg,* and *Paradise Lost.* In the first, Frank Reeves uses the delightful metaphor of the dogs of Rome, leaving us with the image of the dog leading the blind man. This is sufficiently ambiguous for us to be tempted to accuse the author of fence-sitting. The dog, in this role, is both the servant and leader of the disabled man, or is it, perhaps, an example of affectionate symbiosis, a presaging of the environmentally harmonious world that the poet desires? In *Mermaid murdered at Llandanwg*, however, there is no ambiguity. All three conclusions to the story offer violent endings and the reader is left in little doubt that the different forms the violence takes merely reflect the socio-technical developments of the period. An optimistic reading is not possible.

Some clear poetic influences on Frank Reeves's work are readily detectable, and not just those of Tennyson, in *Come into the garden, Myrna,* or Milton, in the aptly named *Paradise Lost,* or Marvell, in *Computer Secrets,* or Arnold, in *Mermaid murdered at Llandanwg.* For me, the poet who is brought to mind is Bertold Brecht, with his accessible rhythms and vocabulary, and contemporary and political subject matter. Brecht was fond of picking up items from the popular press, as well as writing about his experiences of work. We can see Brecht's style and subject matter in poems such as W*oman scarecrow* and *Easter resurrection,* with their almost prose-like rhythms and bland use of the horrific, bereft of analogy.

How will the historically uninformed reader fare with a writer who refers so directly to the politics of his own lifetime? Even with copious notes, can all the references be caught? The notes, perhaps, will act as a barrier to individual interpretation of the poems. Many of the poems are replete with knowledge arising from the lived and studied experience of twentieth-century political life: *The death of Enoch Powell, Frozen objects: an autobiography,* to name but two. Yet this insistence that poetry can address contemporary issues, as well as so-called universal experiences, is an important means of countering one view of romanticism: that poetry is solely about the apparently universal themes of love and loss, themselves refracted through historically-specific fact.

Nevertheless, some of the most successful verses arise from Frank Reeves's reflection on the age-old poetic theme of love. Frank seems to be particularly exercised by the question of whether sex is, or should be, primarily to reinforce romantic love, or to pleasure us. *Come into the garden, Myrna* explicitly addresses this theme and, because it is so deliberately contrasted with Tennyson's original *Come into the garden, Maud,* we might be forgiven for thinking that Frank favours the pleasure principle. But then, we would have had to accept the authenticity of the emotions expressed by Tennyson. This reader, so distanced in values from those expressed in the nineteenth-century poem, has her doubts. We hope that women and men, when forming emotional relationships, never behaved in such an artificial, stereotypical and insincere manner. Frank's verse does more than merely contrast with the earlier poem: it interrogates both views of sexuality. And love of the beloved companion shines through the delightfully amusing *Racist Graffiti* and the gentle and touching *Breast cancer*.

Unsurprisingly, given Frank's interest in social structure and forms, he enjoys the constraints, nay battle, with regular verse form as found in *Quality Control,* with its pivotal central verse that is constructed around the image of the rock or buttress. The image supports the theme as the verse supports the poem. This structure is reinforced by the strict adherence to the same line form throughout the poem. Furthermore, he tends towards an acceptance of other more conventional forms of poetic discourse. He often uses regular metrical patterns as in *Driving angrily to change the world* and *Black woman quartet*.

He does, of course, favour internal rhythms over rhymed line endings. This slightly looser approach to poetic form is well suited to his subject matter - his preference for direct reference to the material world. These internal rhythms make the verse more accessible. In *Strictly an interpretation*, each verse starts with a fast drive, gradually slowing down, reflecting the overall theme of doubt about the narrator's lifework. The imagery in this poem is simple and effective, using readily accessible urban themes of beer and the pub backroom to tease out a complex moral question. Accessible imagery characterises *The milk of human kindness,* except that this utilises a key element of the rural economy, the coco palm, to explore fundamental aspects of human relations.

Many of Frank's strongest poems are those that are most closely linked to narrative. The use of narrative encourages simplicity and forces the spare use of language, with descriptive language serving to drive the story forward. Verses, such as those in *Sawoniuk of British Rail* and *The milk of human kindness,* are all the more effective because the reader is gripped by the events and hurries to the end, seeking the almost cliffhanging conclusion. Frank also uses narrative to explore more formal theories, so that *Being at that time* can be read as a story of an encounter in a forest, or as an exploration of Heidegger's ideas on the meaning of Being.

Some of Frank Reeves's titles are masterly, for example, the unexpected connection of the notorious Sawoniuk to British Rail, the multiple meanings in *Castaway*, and the frightening perspective on death and unemployment in *Bereavement in bright colours*. Perhaps unexpectedness is the lasting impression made on the reader of this collection of poems – the range of subject matter, the freshness and humour of the imagery, the wonderful narratives, the integrity of the themes, and the sheer celebration of human diversity.

Introduction

by Dr Swaran Chandan

Poetry of substance

Frank Reeves is a name that was made known to me by my closest friend, Niranjan Singh Noor, now deceased. It only dawned on me that Frank was a poet – a poet of substance – when he handed over to me a typed manuscript of poetry and asked me to browse through it and to write this introduction. Studying his poetry has been an enchanting experience for me, a new experience, in that this poetry dwells on the presumption that an expectant reader must be knowledgeable, quick-witted, analytical, a good decoder, a linguist, imaginative beyond visible horizons, and a student of philosophy, with ample understanding of materialism, existentialism, socialism and, of course, the science of change in the context of the predicament caused by the crumbling of the socialist states.

In short, Frank's poetry is highly demanding. A reader who is used to reading lightweight verses would do better to stay away from it. Frank's poetry challenges, deviates, shakes, disturbs and breaks asunder your ready-made patterns of thought, perception and cognition. You are burdened with an overdose of thought-provoking material, a complexity of language, unusual metaphors, allegorical structures, bloated signs, and quintessential paraphrases, but yet the polyphony persists and, if rightly understood, the layers of meaning can be laid bare.

In this anthology you don't meet one Frank Reeves but many: a painter who paints portraits as well as landscapes; a narrator with vibrant story-telling skills; a voluptuous lover who penetrates deep into the soul and cells of his beloved; a wanderer who lets no opportunity slip away to make the most of his adventures; an indignant anti-racist who uses the occasion to rebuke the racist without losing the subtlety of the poetic word; a rebel who snatches every inch of ground from under the feet of traditionalists to go as far as to justify the acid observations of Nietzsche. Frank is a philosopher who digs deep into the theory in which critical social practices are embedded to mock his own pedestal, as well as the position of others who, in the passage of time and with much wasted energy, had come to desire an undisturbed peaceful settlement because the revolution of which they once dreamed had been swept away like a glass-house in a torrential storm of gigantic stones.

Hegel be damned, it was Kant and later, Croche, who pleaded the autonomy of the plane of expression. The Marxist philosophers and critics, however, showed

6 Introduction

preference for the conceptual plane, thereby reducing the expression to the concept, or, the signifier to the signified, thus limiting the possibility of interpreting poetry as language-beyond-language, pregnant with multiple meanings, and capable of renewed interpretation, generation after generation. There is no one-to-one meaning in art, especially in poetry.

Let's study some of Frank's poems to perceive the magic of his signification in producing meanings. Frank has divided his anthology into ten sections according to the poems' subject matter. He has done this to help the reader concentrate wholeheartedly on the parameters of a particular theme and to break sharply with others. In this way, he provides clues to solving the mysteries of comprehension. He also takes the trouble to supply a little background information to some of the poems, just in case the reader is unfamiliar with a certain character, context, or consequence. For some of his poems, such acquaintance is crucial, for the reader might happen to read only poetry and be unfamiliar with the disciplines of social science and philosophy.

Black woman quartet

In the section *Black woman quartet*, the poet paints four pictorial images of black womanhood. In *Black woman in the night sky*, the poet imagines the form of a black woman lying recumbent in the void of the sky and wishes that she would descend to earth so that he might discover her firm dark body. The process of discovery would conceal the emptiness of night and fill his emotional void.

In *Black woman at dawn*, the poet dreams of a black woman bedecked in cobweb pearls in a milk-dipped dawn, only to recognise that predatory forces, symbolised by a domestic cat, have destroyed a fond relationship.

In *Black woman at noon*, the poet visualises a black silhouette against the blinding sun, which resembles his black beloved, then goes on to recollect their moments of love which, despite the racial hatred of society, persists because of their faith in one another. *In Black woman at sunset,* the poet imparts new meaning to the day and night in terms of visibility and non-visibility, love and hatred, a rising and a setting sun. But love must make its own clear light, like a glow-worm, as 'pastel' promises are doomed to fade and be forgotten.

Garden poems

There are six poems in the *garden* section of this book. The first, *Woman scarecrow,* is a narrative poem that describes the creation of a female scarecrow, only for it to be sexually molested and raped in broad daylight. When its eyes are gouged out by pigeons, it collapses, wide legged across a flower pot, crying out with words partly borrowed from the Bible, ' Oh mother, why have you forsaken me?' The poet establishes that the creator of any creation cannot always foresee the consequences of her own creation. It could well be observed at this point that, soon after its creation, a poem breaks away from its creator, leaving us to interpret, enjoy, or cast it aside as we might choose. That was why some literary critics announced 'the death of the author'. Frank, himself, stresses that his poetry must live or die independently of him (see: *About the author*).

The other five poems in the section address the pains, tensions and conflicts of sexual love. Violence and sudden shafts of light illuminate the consequences of conformity to social norms in relationships. In *Garden ornament*, the poetic he buys a rustic statue from a garden shop and adorns his garden with its life-sized nakedness. As he watches it from within the family home, however, the bare-breasted and petrified statue reminds him of the consequences of choosing a monogamous lifestyle. Similarly, in *Gladioli*, the poet portrays the idea that love sometimes does not lie in snipping flower heads but in leaving them intact. Rejection, as well as the retention of pure beauty, invites us to leave the gladioli unpicked. In *Behind the hedge*, neighbours gather the fallen fruits of love in their gardens. One couple uses the hedge as a double shield to hide both their sexual contentment and knowledge of their neighbour's predicament. She is bruised and fallen fruit, emotionally and physically injured in her relationship.

When we write poetry we treat language cruelly, in the sense that we deviate from the linguistic norms. We give new meanings to the existing words, or denude them of their ordinary meanings. If a poet cannot play with words in this fashion, then his/her poetry leaves a lot to be desired. It is, in fact, a distortion of ordinary language to transform it into poetic language. Frank's poetry is full of such distortions, cruelties and deviations. Let us take, for example, *Come into the garden Myrna*. This and many other poems in the collection are a combination of narrative poetry, portrait painting, landscape and pictorial imagery, plus penetrating moral commentary. This poem starts with the description of a pulsating party at which the poetic I is attracted to Myrna by a gesture of the hips, and then:

> As night flies sweep like fighters
> To strafe the battle lanterns
> Beamed down on clinging couples,
> We talk and drink canned lager,
> Exploring with pink tendrils
> The terms of our attraction.

8 Introduction

'Pink tendrils' stand for the fingers of human hands. The 'terms of attraction' constitute the pivotal concept around which the whole poem has been structured. And, in order to uncover the innermost feelings of the duo, a metaphor of petals, black slugs and hunger has been devised.

> As we stroll, we comment how
> A rose's fallen petals
> Attract the black slugs, hungry
> To browse on fading beauty.
> You seem more aware than I
> That every moment's precious.

Similarly, the hunger for sex, 'quixotic hope', is represented as a sweet pea 'among winged insects, brushing moist pistils'. The whole scene is set for the drive towards foreplay, proceeding to final play, or the bursting of 'the swollen pod of life'. The poetic I becomes emotionally involved by their love-making: 'a spotted frog …dives with my feelings into deep water', but Myrna insists that the encounter was only for a moment's pleasure with no promises made. The poetic I observes wryly:

> How I wish our transaction
> Could be described prettily
> In the lies of a poet,
> Avoiding sordid matters
> Such as your mudded costume
> And brevity of ardour.

The New Jerusalem

Ever since the Russian revolution of October 1917, followed by the Second World War and the division of Europe into two, Marxism declined progressively as a social science, being treated instead as a cult, or gospel truth, which was beyond question. Unlike the natural sciences, the social sciences, no matter how sophisticated, are never as precise or powerfully predictive as the former. Personally, I find an analysis of the development of human society (historical materialism) and the application of the laws of development (dialectical materialism) both helpful and enlightening, but to presume, therefore, that the workers will one day turn the world upside-down, and change it for the better, is no more than an act of fortune-telling. You can analyse what is given but cannot tell what the future has in store, especially when the given history bears no witness to it. At the most you can offer a series of possibilities and probabilities, none of which may occur. Orthodox Marxists, if any are still left, insist that it is not Marxism that has failed, but the application of it. This is like saying that the teachings of the Bible are perfectly true, but that they can't be made to work in practice. This is what cultism is about.

To return to a theme of Frank's poetry, it does not matter so much that Marxism as a philosophy of change has failed, as does the fact that thousands of sincere workers, who struggled so hard to bring about a better world, appear to have sacrificed their lives in vain. A belief system that promised abolition of the state and the end of exploitation created a state with even greater power to dominate and exploit the workers. The counter-revolutions didn't fall out of the blue. Every edifice based on such cultist behaviour must fall and so too did this one. Frank Reeves is well aware of the impact of these events and his poems, such as *Geraniums, Strictly an interpretation, Driving angrily to change the world*, and *Frozen objects: an autobiography*, deal splendidly with the practical and emotional issues involved in a language which is subtle, engrossing, transcendent and metaphorical. Just look at these lines from *Geraniums*:

> By such relentless giving of the self
> They strove to build their New Jerusalem.
> More humble now with age, he takes his trowel
> To weed a blossoming utopia.
>
> The noble cause of labour was their aim,
> No need to bode a futile consequence.

Issues of race

Five important poems are included in the section entitled *Issues of race*: *I'm a Jew, The death of Enoch Powell, Sawoniuk of British Rail, Racist graffiti* and *Niranjan Singh Noor*. Although much can be said and written about these poems, I shall confine myself to examining only two of them.

Frank began to write about Enoch Powell after watching his funeral on television. On being asked by his mixed-race child, 'Who was Enoch Powell?', the poet begins to shake with fury, fury at the damage done to ethnic minority families and to the relationship between the races by this xenophobe in the aftermath of his notorious 'rivers of blood' speech in 1968. The poet goes on to pinpoint Powell's fundamental conviction (either misconceived or knowingly adopted for political reasons) that racial groups must always live in a hostile relationship to one another. The poet is bitterly opposed to the 'pale lily platitudes' uttered that day by British statesmen of all hues and pours scorn on the short memories of the 'great statesmen' who had so conveniently forgotten the grief that Powell had caused to ethnic minorities living in Britain at that time. The poet describes the way that he, his black wife, and ethnic minority people generally, suffered the consequences of Powell's polarising oratory. The poet also expresses his fear of 'dormant animosities' arising once more to the surface and of Powell's name being invoked again by statesman to appease their hunger for power.

Frank starts his poem about Niranjan Singh Noor with an account of how they first met. They became friends while drinking tea served up on 'a steel tray of politics'. Such a tray never bends; it can only be broken and replaced with an alternative political creed, something the poet knows with absolute certainty that his resolute friend would never agree to. The poem describes the Indian workers' struggle on the picket lines, unsupported by the white workers, who are referred to in a British imperial context as a labour 'aristocracy'. The white workers, under the false impression that their jobs might be stolen, hated their Indian comrades. Yet, says the poet, Noor sought class unity and demanded equal rights for both blacks and whites. Frank, Noor's friend and ally, laments the death of this fearless Sikh and fighter-poet, who saw the human race as one and indivisible. The ever-hopeful poet weaves an illusion of meeting Noor, the 'enlightener', to shape out yet another victory.

Philosophical inspiration

Frank's four poems, inspired by philosophical themes, especially *Being at that time,* and *Community (tribute to Nietzsche),* appear to be aimed at the intellectual, although they can be understood and enjoyed simply at the level of their natural imagery. *Being at that time* explores Martin Heidegger's philosophy of being against the background of his active membership of the German national socialist party, with its anti-semitic ideology.

Community (tribute to Nietzsche) delves into the various meanings of community, challenging the cosy assumption that it supports and succours its members. This community breaks shop windows, swears at the passers-by when they 'jettison the junk of mores, modes and marriages', and exposes itself to women in the park, yet it is worshipped as a secular god, for god is dead. Frank seems to be agreeing with Friedrich Nietzsche's aphorism that 'morality is the herd instinct in the individual'. The poet's eye remains on the ignorant traditional conservative herd instinct characteristic of the crowd, and dissociates itself sharply from the idealistic concept of community subscribed to by officialdom.

Strictly an interpretation is the poem I like most in this section, firstly, because the phenomenon of change in nature (evolution) is inevitable and secondly, because the phenomenon of forced change by human interference (revolution) is not supported by historical evidence. Thus, the end result is that, despite our repeated efforts to change the world so that the workers become the rulers, we have spent time only in interpreting the world.

Caribbean themes

The milk of human kindness is yet another narrative poem that has been very skilfully composed. The literary competence of the poet can be judged from the fact that his similes and metaphors are all selected from the harsh reality of the life that the characters are forced to live. Granville's old mother's routine existence cannot rightly be depicted without reference to her surroundings: the coco palm, the three-legged stool, etc. Granville's tragic end, or something like it at the emotional level, may be a fate shared by many who emigrate for a major part of their lives and then return as strangers to their place of birth. I remember a poem in Panjabi, which goes:

> Those who have gone to foreign lands
> To earn their bread and butter, will
> If ever they return, bask at
> Their mother's funeral, or
> Occupy a space in the graveyard.

Townscape

In the *Townscape* section, Frank tells the story of a 'castaway' who lives alone on a traffic island in 'roaring solitude', hiding himself, as 'a shell-shocked victim of an ancient war', in the 'wreckage of the mind'. He is watched by frustrated motorists, stuck in traffic jams. The poet yearns to be like the vagrant, steering his own destiny alone, 'no longer moored by social anchor chains'.

Ave Maria is another powerful poem, this time about a pregnant prostitute forced out to sell herself on the eve of giving birth. The sordid context of the resultant nativity is vividly portrayed and an inevitable parallel drawn with the birth of the Christ child. This poem is a strong satire on modernism and a substantial reminder that despite our material achievements, we have made little moral progress in two thousand years. It is a well-knit and beautiful poem and, if it were not for keeping myself to a word limit, I would have quoted it in full, but that isn't necessary as it's there to read in the book. I don't want to quote it in part, lest you should lose sight of its fullness and careful construction.

Friends, family and self

Frank Reeves was unemployed for some time and knows very well the pain of joblessness. He has depicted this, most revealingly, in *Bereavement in bright colours.* The poet attends the funeral of a man he does not know and begins to feel that he himself is the dead man. To be unemployed is to lose one's identity as a person, and a jobless person is as good as dead.

The last poem I want to talk about is *Driving angrily to change the world.* This is actually the poem of every one of us who once embarked upon the highway of revolution to change the world. The 'mind was sharp and body muscular and slim', the eyes full of anger, and the world around unfair and unjust. The dream was to knock it down and rebuild it according to our own rules. The road seemed 'intellectually straight' and the revolution not far ahead. But after a long drive forward, we discover that the route is much longer and more crooked than we ever imagined when we set out. So we stop for a coffee, but not just that: a career and a family. Ignoring distractions, we resume the journey. The traffic of revolution continues, but at a snail's pace. We try to overtake the traffic but find that millions of people are mangled in the grim wreckage of capitalism. The world has not been changed: instead, it has changed us. Frank has written this poem from the driving seat and thus fully comprehends the minds of all those people who once strove to change the world to make an impossible dream come true, but failed and became disillusioned, with the more stubborn and intractable becoming mangled in the wreckage.

Conclusion

I have only touched on some of the poems, which merit, and could readily sustain, a prolonged analysis and commentary. There are many more dimensions, which need grasping, analysing and decoding. But an introduction of this kind has its own limitations. And I, too, have mine.

Frank's poetry has really impressed me. It makes you sit down and think. You can't just flick and shuffle the pages and reach the end. No. Each poem grips you and compels you to listen to it, catch it and enjoy it and take its imprint away for ever to haunt you. It is thought-provoking poetry, like that of Niranjan Singh Noor. I wish he were alive and we – Noor, Frank and I – had read this book together, discussed it, and gone to bed with the satisfaction that, although we could not change the world, we definitely had achieved something in the process. However, be it as it is, I thank you, Frank, for letting me be the first reader of this collection, for there will be thousands of others when the book is published.

BLACK WOMAN QUARTET

Black woman in the night sky

On cloudless nights, when you are far away,
I see, recumbent on a quilted void,
Your sable shape marked out by sparkling stars,
Across an aching loneliness of sky.
Towards my gaze, consolingly, you tilt
The curving constellation of your thighs:
Your breasts, full-tipped by nipple pricks of light,
Your eyes, two orbs of glinting anthracite.

If Greeks can set their pallid heroines
On crystal spheres until the end of time,
Then you, incarnate, can descend to earth
And I shall know your body, black and firm.
Our passion, for a while, will burn so bright
It may conceal the emptiness of night.

Black woman at dawn

A pale ray penetrates the puckered drapes
And strikes the empty pillow by my side.
Awakened by a witching light, I rise
And from the window scan the milk-dipped dawn.
The foxy shadows on the lawn obscure
The raven lustre of a woman's form,
Yet there, bedecked in cobweb pearls, you stand,
A presence conjured at my heart's command.

We listened long ago to morning birds
And watched the vibrant hues of day dispel
The nightshade of impending separateness.
Since then, the cat that prowls beneath the hedge
Has pounced upon my plumpest dream of you
And left a trail of feathers in the dew.

Black woman at noon

At noon, when staring blankly into space,
I visualise your shapely silhouette,
Intensely black, against the blinding sun.
Loose-limbed and naked on the coral sand,
You dance, erect, with breasts and hips asway,
And coming close, you hold me in your arms.
The after-image of that day lives on
Long after the reality has gone.

We entered once a crucible of love
And walked through waves of molten gold.
The heartless enemies of black and white
Stoked up the furnace flames to burn us both.
While faith allowed us to survive the heat,
A dying fire would signal our defeat.

Black woman at sunset

The shining mare of day that pranced with us
Across the azure pastures of the sky
Lies wounded on the bladed hills and bleeds
A crimson river on night's altar slab.
Smeared in the heart-spilt plasma of our love,
We search each other's face, yours black, mine white,
Until the failing sun is plagued with doubt
And grudgeful night crows peck our bright eyes out.

My fiery fancy of you dies away:
Your dazzling smile on lips, full formed, has set.
Since you have gone, the air is still and sad
And the dismal world is inconsolable.
Like glow-worms, we must make our own clear light,
For pastel promises will fade at night.

GARDEN POEMS

A Woman Scarecrow

Because no-one had heard of scarepigeons,
Mel made a scarecrow for the allotment
To frighten away pigeons from her peas.

As women can be terrifying, too,
Mel decided on a woman scarecrow.

The skeleton was fashioned from bean sticks,
Tied with unobtrusive green garden twine,
But the head was not a garden product
Like an old turnip, prone to decay,
But a manikin torso, rescued from
A fashionable hairdresser's in town.

Its oval face was painted carefully
In house paint to highlight the bright bean eyes,
With a touch of real lipstick to the lips.

Two plastic bottles provided the breasts,
With erect screw tops aroused as nipples.

The scarecrow's appearance was completed
With a blond Afro wig, and a fur coat
Which had been cast off by the fashion world
Out of respect for animal welfare.

Among the peas, the female scarecrow was not
Inclined to anti-social behaviour
And this soon became known to the pigeons.

Attracted also by her elegance,
They would swoop down, some pecking at pea plants,
Others settling on her head, arms and breasts.

This well-endowed and well-dressed woman, left
Standing alone in a deserted place,
Was soon sexually molested by
A male scarecrow and raped in broad daylight.

As no complaint was lodged with the police,
The crime was never investigated.

Shortly after her horrific ordeal,
The pigeons returned to gouge out her eyes,
Destroying her sight and scarring her face.

She sits on a flower pot, wide legged as on
A water closet, grimacing blindly
At the sky, crying out in a loud voice,
"Oh mother, why have you forsaken me?"

Mel, as maker, holding herself to blame
For the unfortunate turn of events,
Can't look her damaged creature in the eye.

Paradoxically, having just lost both
Her innocence and beauty, the scarecrow,
With a dead pigeon tangled in her wig,
Proceeds to fulfil her primary purpose.

Though design is a feature intrinsic
To scarecrow genesis, do not assume
That, even with the best laid plans, creators
Will always foresee the consequence.

Garden ornament

When examining the rustic statues
In the garden shop, he concludes, with some
Sincerity, that her slender body
Is more graceful and better proportioned
Than the resin Venus pouring water
From an amphora into a scallop.
He would prefer, he explains, to adorn
His landscape with her life-sized nakedness.
Her eyes are founts of sorrow, now. Is she
To be some petrified embellishment,
Condemned to stand bare-breasted on the lawn,
While he admires her from the family home?

Behind the hedge

We gather fallen apples from our lawn.
Next door, the neighbours harvest purple plums.
One day, when we'd made love beneath the tree,
And lay, contented, on the picnic rug,
We heard loud quarrelling behind the hedge.
Later, we spied by chance our neighbour with
Her eye, inflamed. She turned away in shame.
We hoped she hadn't heard our fun and guessed
She had no wish for us to know her pain.
The privet, dense enough for birds, does not
Conceal our deeds, but lets us feign instead
An ignorance of bruised and fallen fruit.

Come into the garden, Myrna

I meet you by chance late on
A sultry August evening,
At a party pulsating
To electronic rhythms,
Like a fat caterpillar
Of reciprocal segments.

I see you in the parlour,
My dazzled eyes dilating
In rapt appreciation
Of your smooth-flowing movement.
Turning your hips toward me,
You invite me by smiling.

You sway your body, supple
In a chic dress, revealing
Your long straight back, nestling a
Tattooed moth between shoulders
Smooth to the touch and softly
Sheened in the subdued lighting.

As night flies sweep like fighters
To strafe the battle lanterns
Beamed down on clinging couples,
We talk and drink canned lager,
Exploring with pink tendrils
The terms of our attraction.

The patio window opens
On a terrace at twilight,
Enveloped in a perfume
Of smoke and honeysuckle.
Oh, come with me quietly
Into the garden, Myrna.

As we stroll, we comment how
A rose's fallen petals
Attract the black slugs, hungry
To browse on fading beauty.
You seem more aware than I
That every moment's precious.

But in the smirking summer,
Gravid with mawkish nectar,
Love's meant to last for ever,
With quixotic hope soaring
Like a sweet pea among winged
Insects brushing moist pistils.

We grip each other tightly,
Oblivious of flowers
And the scent of lavender,
Supplanted by Givenchy,
Sprayed behind ear lobes, tender
To wide unfettered kisses.

Then naked on the flattened
Lawn, silk pants cast carelessly
Aside, we burst the swollen
Pod of life, disturbing a
Spotted frog, which dives with my
Feelings into deep water.

Placated with our passion,
We leave behind its debris:
Those strange metallic mushrooms,
Beer cans on the rockery,
And a dead fish, the condom
Floating among pond lilies.

But still I love you, Myrna,
Beyond the garden gate to
Starkly real eternity,
Where desperate bats, as blind as
We, hurtle towards heaven
Through unpretentious darkness.

Aware of the romantic
By your side, you grow wary,
Insisting our encounter
Was for a moment's pleasure
And that you made no promise
In the damp of the garden.

How I wish our transaction
Could be described prettily
In the lies of a poet,
Avoiding sordid matters,
Such as your mudded costume
And brevity of ardour.

Gladioli

In Autumn, the gladioli
Protrude towards a gloomy sky -
Erect stems of garnet red that
Dominate the border. With the
Careful preparation of an
Executioner, expertly,
He snips the spikes, gathering them
Into a bouquet to present
To her in vain expectation
That she will welcome his display.
Like skilfully embalmed corpses,
Cut flowers are already dead.

Geraniums

Retired now, my comrade, the old fire brand,
Sits alert on his garden wheelbarrow,
Admiring his geraniums, scarlet
In Autumn, like the flag of socialism.
Marshalled in their earthen beds, the flowers shed
Their petal tears, like martyrs' blood congealed
Upon the path of primal memory:
The Paris commune and the barricades,
Protesters massacred in Petrograd,
In Spain, the workers shot by Franco's troops.
As red confetti mingles with the grass,
I sense the pent-up anger in his heart
And know he could not let a fascist pass.
When horses charged the miners' picket lines,
He showed no fear and firmly stood his ground,
Uniting with the workers of the world
To share the easy flowing of their wounds.
By such relentless giving of the self,
They strove to build their new Jerusalem.
More humble now with age, he takes his trowel
To weed a blossoming utopia.
In hindsight, was their sacrifice in vain?
Through understanding him, I cannot ask.
The noble cause of labour was their aim,
No need to bode a futile consequence.
He looks me in the eye, suspiciously,
Then wheels the barrow off along the path,
Leaving behind the ghost of sweated toil:
The pungent scent of crushed geranium,
And petal stains upon the paving slabs.

ISSUES OF RACE

I'm a Jew

With my dark suit and unkempt beard,
I'm asked outright at a party,
In front of friends, if I'm a Jew.
Bemused by a simple question
I didn't expect, I reply,
With curious rapidity,
"Not to my knowledge", adding, as
A joke, "but I *am* circumcised!"
My bottle-blonde inquisitor
Smirks, unenthusiastically.
Guessing at her predilection
(Has she discerned my high sex drive,
Fine intellect and business flair?),
I try to be more positive,
Adopting the stratagem that,
Indeed, I'm a Yiddisher boy:
One with liberal views, powerful car
And a large house in Golders Green.

Yet in the truth of that moment,
Was there a reservation trapped
In a rats' nest, deep in the sewer
Between medieval history
And the Nazis' grim holocaust?
Or was I, as gentile, merely
Affirming the reality
Of my ancestral relations?
What, proud of being British, me?
I never had a say in it.
The roots of these demented views
Are more intrusive than we think.
What sense to give to pride or shame
In our genetic destiny?
I need to stand up every day
And say, when asked to give my name,
I'm Spartacus, I'm Malcolm X,
And just as much, I'm Abraham.

The death of Enoch Powell

Enoch Powell (1912 to 1998) was elected as a Conservative Member of Parliament for Wolverhampton in 1950, serving as Minister of Health in the Macmillan government in 1960 and in Heath's shadow cabinet. In 1968, his "river of blood" speech on the perils of immigration to Britain led to a climate of racial excitement and to the vilification of black people from the Indian subcontinent, the Caribbean and elsewhere in the New Commonwealth. Powell, a former brigadier in the army in India, advocated "re-emigration" and opposed anti-discrimination legislation. When he died in 1998, politicians of both Left and Right paid tribute to his statesmanship.

ജ്ഞ

Seeing his funeral on the news
With tributes paid by great statesmen,
You ask me "who was Enoch Powell?"
I look across our living room
At you, my golden daughter, child
Produced by parents, black and white.
And even now, when thirty years
Have passed, I shake with fury at
The damage caused to families, such
As ours, by that old xenophobe.

Like the twin barrels of a gun,
His penetrating eyes preside
With arrogant self-confidence
Over the false assertion that
The races dwell in enmity.
Recalling Powell's pronouncement now,
Should we regret, as others do,
His passing in old age and, conscious
Of his life's work, strew pale lily
Platitudes upon his grave?

How short the memories of those
Who speak with lavish deference of
His outstanding contribution
To our politics, but ignore
Conveniently, it seems, his grand
Apocalyptic vision of
" A river foaming with much blood",
The portent of that racial strife
Which would ensue if immigrants
Resided in our neighbourhood.

Identified as enemies,
We felt it then, our *Kristallnacht:*
Graffiti on the synagogue,
The children spat upon at school,
A turban taken from a Sikh,
Black people beaten in the street,
And when your parents walked through town
The crowd would glare in disbelief,
Some shrieking: "mongreliser",
"Traitor to the race", and "nigger whore".

Such small personal matters, these,
Of no consequence to a man
Who believed the driving purpose
Of a politician was the
Dramatic presentation of
A polarised predicament.
You'd have been to him just one more
"Wide-eyed grinning piccaninny",
A number whose arrival meant
Destruction for his way of life.

But even as his word-storm burst,
Intensities of love still surged
Like bright electric arcs across
Sullen distrustful distances.
And men and women, scorning Powell's
Pronouncements on identity,
Squeezed hands between the colour bars.
Child, born of interracial fire,
Your life negates the rhetoric
Of synthetic separateness.

But though your world is fine with friends,
The times can change as day to night,
And dormant animosities
Emerge like fungus on the walls
Of rotting tenements where youths
Sit round begrudging those with jobs.
Rolling their black shirts back, they shoot
Cheap jingo drugs in flesh tattooed
With prejudice, then strut with flags
Behind the pall of destiny.

Capricious men in uniform
Heap up "the nation's funeral pyre".
For those uncertain times to come,
Please keep a sharp machete of
The mind in readiness for when
The social ground gives way and the
Grimacing corpse of Enoch Powell,
Invoked by statesmen for their ends,
Arises from its tomb to speak
Once more for all those little folk.

Sawoniuk of British Rail

Britain's first war crimes trial led to the conviction in 1999 of Anthony Sawoniuk, aged 78, a former British Rail ticket collector, living in Bermondsey, south-east London. He was found guilty of the murder, fifty-seven years earlier, of eighteen Jews in Domachevo, his home town in Belarus, in the former Soviet Union. As a poor peasant, known as Andrusha, he had joined the police force set up under the German occupation and had risen rapidly in the ranks to play an enthusiastic role in hunting down escaping Jews. Elderly eyewitnesses from Domachevo, such as Alexander Baglay, aged 69, Fedora Yakimuk, aged 72, and Fedor Dan, aged 75, were flown to London to testify. I am indebted to the trial reports in *The Guardian* (3.3.1999, 6.3.1999, 2.4.1999) and *The Mirror* (2.4.1999).

৪৩৫৪

You'd never have noticed the man
In uniform who collected
Your ticket as you left the train.
His grim history was hidden
By humdrum manual work in the
Confusing aftermath of war.

From his bearing, you'd imagine
He'd exercise authority
Effectively, ensuring that
Standard ticket holders who sat
In first-class accommodation
Were sent to their part of the train.

So difficult to believe that,
Long ago, in the dark forest
Of a war-ravaged Belarus,
He vied with German soldiers in
The routine task of catching Jews,
Selecting thousands to be shot.

Sawoniuk of British Rail, now
Retired, denied he was the same
Young man, known to the people of
Domachevo as Andrusha,
The butcher, and assured the court
That many of his friends were Jews.

But one twelve-year-old boy,
Caught scavenging in the ghetto,
Witnessed the police commandant
Take two Jewish men and a woman
To a pit, freshly dug in sand,
Where he ordered them to undress.

The woman, out of modesty,
Declined to remove underwear
Until threatened with a beating.
When all three were naked, Andrusha
Shot them cleanly through the neck,
Somewhat like punching a ticket.

Fedora Yakimuk told how,
While reaping, she cut herself with
A sickle. The wound was bandaged
With a rag soaked in iodine,
Staining her sleeve yellow like the
Armband the Jews were forced to wear.

Andrusha and a German mistook
Her for a Jew and dragged her off
To be shot. "He knew me so well",
She said, "but didn't protect me.
It was the German who inspected
The dressing and let me go".

You can't help but think Sawoniuk
Might have been less than competent
In his duties for British Rail.
Would travellers have been directed
To the right train, or arrived at
Their intended destination?

Transfer of skill often proves hard
In the anonymous concourse
Of an estranged experience,
Where human beings are equipped
With ticket pliers or pistols
To demonstrate proficiency.

Was the diabetic pensioner,
Raising his steel-rimmed spectacles
To wipe away his tears, really
The same swaggering policeman
Who'd seized the chance to settle scores
Against his more wealthy neighbours?

Or had the youthful memories
Of witnesses, like their bodies,
Become warped and twisted with age,
Resulting in an induced, but
False, identification of
A faceless ticket collector?

After describing the killings,
Alexander Baglay confirmed
Under cross-examination
Sawoniuk was there: " I recall
It perfectly", he declared, and
The jury believed his story.

In recognising the unknown
Ticket collector as the man
Who'd menaced their community,
The people of Domachevo
Gave Sawoniuk back what he'd lost:
His own moral identity.

Enthusiastically, he chose
To join an organisation
Whose purpose reflected his own.
The worst crimes are committed when
Tickets are punched, instructions aren't
Questioned and the trains run on time.

Racist graffiti

"Whitey yu daf[1]"and "nigga ye dead",
Phonetic familiarities,
Scrawled with felt tip on the subway walls.

What subterranean sentiments,
Fanned by "NF[2] rules" and "black is best",
Fuel the fight for last-word dominance!

Vile secrets explode beneath the road,
Like farts stinking, but strangely silent,
Tightly squeezed in polite company.

And worse, the last taboo, whispered as
Bawdy bar joke, the phallus-focussed
Sexual nightmare: a black Priapus[3],

Overwhelmed by white Shelah-na-Gig[4],
Vagina screaming (by Edvard Munch[5],
Or, more likely, an Eddy, or Skunk),

Drawn from life by horny teenagers,
Fooling promiscuously at dusk
With the crude mysteries of the occult.

Cave painting of the primitive kind,
No innuendo, just underlined,
Offending our public decency,

Yet remaining there, never removed,
Neither by steam jet, nor from memory,
Deep-throat, but still ejaculated.

How those stubborn fantasies reveal
Their secret selves in naive frescoes,
Daubed by natural expressionists.

Be thankful the future's fly-posted:
Black man and white woman, clasping hands
Gently enraptured and respectful,

Walking through the obscene underpass
Of stale cultural interference,
Noticing only one another.

Though pissed on perceptively by drunks,
This modern art has little impact
When "get-real attraction rules, OK!"

---

[1] 'daft' or stupid.
[2] National Front (Right-wing political party).
[3] Priapus was a Roman fertility god, usually portrayed with a large erect phallus.
[4] A Shelah na Gig is a vaginally-explicit female figure carved in stone on ancient churches, especially in Ireland.
[5] Reference to the Norwegian artist, Edvard Munch, and his famous painting *The Scream*.

Niranjan Singh Noor (1933–1999)

Niranjan Singh Noor was born on the 6th January 1933 in the district of the Panjab known as Montgomery in what is now Pakistan. He came to Wolverhampton, England, in 1965, at the age of 32. He worked as a labourer in Cannon Industries, as a postman, a teacher, and a race equality adviser, retiring in 1997 as the Director of Community Education at Bilston Community College. I first met him when he was National President of the Indian Workers' Association, a radical union of immigrants from the Indian sub-continent, many of whom worked in appalling conditions in the local foundries and factories.

We campaigned together for multi-cultural education in the face of a local authority wedded to narrow assimilationist policies. Noor repeatedly exposed the then widespread racial discrimination against black and Asian pupils in the schools and the official neglect and suppression of minority cultures, exemplified by the Grove Junior School turban case in which a head teacher sent home an eleven-year-old boy for wearing a turban to school. Noor played a leading role in the Turban Action Group and was subsequently sued for libel by the head teacher when he called him a racist. Noor lost the case and had to pay a sum well in excess of £50,000.

Within the Indian community, Noor was a much-esteemed poet, famous for his great epic in Panjabi about the life of Ho Chi Minh. When he died suddenly after an asthma attack on the 3rd June 1999, the community lost a civil rights leader, educator and poet. I lost a brave and loyal friend, who deeply inspired me and my writing. His cause lives on in the legacy of his fine poetry and the successes of his political struggle.

I was honoured to recite the following lament at Noor's funeral service on the 11 June 1999, in the Sedgley Street Gurdwara, Wolverhampton and again at the commemorative meeting of the Progressive Writers' Association on the 5 September 1999.

The five Ks of the Sikh religion, the kes (hair and beard), kangha (comb), kach (breeches), kara (steel bracelet) and kirpan (sword), provide much of the poem's imagery.

ೞಛ

Somewhere deep in a Midland town,
Shrouded in industrial smog
And clouds of poisonous racism,
We shook hands in the bare front room
Of a bleak red-brick terraced house.

On a steel tray of politics,
You served me a cup of sweet tea,
The *amrit*[1] of a common cause,
Stirred with a spoon and your sharp tongue,
Twirling like a double-edged sword.

Always your eyes, with their glint of
The *kara*, or bracelet, were fixed
On action, as immigrant workers,
In foundries and factories, fought
To reassert their dignity.

Shivering in cotton garments
Beneath acrylic pullovers,
They stood firm on the picket lines
Against an aristocracy
Of insufferable white labour.

Thin lips sucking on cigarettes,
Superiority in doubt,
How they vied to humiliate
Their Indian brothers: the "wogs"
And "stinking coons" who stole their jobs!

Yet, always, you managed to hold
True to the fleeting vision of
Class unity, seeking only
A single rate for black and white,
And to use the same lavatories.

Gaunt, with your beard, or *kes*, spread grey,
Beneath powerful spectacles,
You spoke with thoughtful eloquence
To thousands gathered in the hall
To celebrate their martyrs' day.

You cried out for the children, too,
Cooped in Victorian classrooms,
Seated, subdued, in serried rows,
Before sceptical teachers,
Doubting their capabilities.

When Panjab culture was attacked
And pupils' mother tongue suppressed,
You took the *kangha* comb to school
To separate the strands of truth
From lies and racial prejudice.

Sensitive to family cares,
You roared, angry as a lion,
At the perverse authority
That scorned the *Khalsa*^{2} way of life,
To turn away a turbaned boy.

The pen became your *kirpan* sword
As, dressed in the fine *kach* breeches
Of education, you rode out
To the war of the classes on
A white charger of poetry.

Desperate, as an asthmatic,
To breathe new life into
A political carcass, racked
By suffocating injustice,
You gave that battle all your strength.

For ever challenging a mogul
Despotism of power and greed,
Niranjan Singh Noor, fearless Sikh
And friend, you saw the human race
As one and indivisible.

Our force is weaker now you've gone,
But you've bequeathed an armoury
Of words to your beloved ones:
Those men and women, black and white,
Who clamour for equality.

Somewhere deep in a Midland town,
Beneath a sky of purest red,
Together, we shall drink sweet tea,
And you and I will plot once more
That last illusive victory.

---

[1] the elixir of life: sugar dissolved in water and stirred with a double-edged sword, used in Sikh baptism.

[2] literally, 'the pure ones', referring to the religious community of the Sikhs as founded by Guru Gobind Singh, the tenth guru.

PHILOSOPHICAL INSPIRATION

Being at that time

In 1953, when I was aged eight, my father took me on a tour of Germany and Austria. After a visit to Strasbourg and the cathedral, we entered the Black Forest via Freiburg. My father bought a cuckoo clock, the traditional product of the forest craftsmen.

The poem describes our imaginary encounter in the forest with Martin Heidegger, the philosopher of Being, and member of the National Socialist Party, who owned a chalet (that came to be known as *die hütte*) at Todtnauberg.

Both Edmund Husserl, once professor of philosophy at Freiburg University, and Hannah Arendt, Heidegger's former student and friend, were Jewish. When Jews were purged from public office, Husserl was replaced by Heidegger as rector of the university.

 જીભ્ય

Being at that time a child, ignorant
Of the devastations of history
And intricate methods of argument,
I can recall only his intense eyes,
Sharp moustache and a briskness of manner.

We met a philosopher, my father
And I, when walking in a dark forest.
He seemed far more startled by the fact that
We existed, than by his encounter
With two wanderers, deep in the woods.

Who *we* were was less important than our
Being, or what it was for us to *be*.
In that leafy glade, he saw only our
Vacant shadows, not our vibrant bodies,
Whistling shrill tunes, with rucksacks on our backs.

My father, comfortable with his own
Distinguishing particularities,
Was never convinced that his knowing wink
Should be bracketed apart in order
To ascertain the meaning of Being.

Spreading butter on his pumpernickel,
He challenged the wisdom of abstracting
Humanity, while the philosopher,
Spurning such crassness, insisted on an
Analysis of Being in general.

Yet father, having lived through two world wars,
Was troubled when fir trees were grown in rows
And soldiers strutted by in uniform.
He feared a rigid symmetry of mind
Would cancel individuality.

The philosopher proposed *Dasein¹,* which
Flickered like a sunbeam in the branches,
Before entering the World-with-others.
At times, a canopy of swaying leaves,
Or swirling flags, blocked out its feeble light.

Like a young child abandoned in the woods,
The innocence of Being could be snared
By cackling witches and imprisoned in
A castle of Aryan mystery,
Policed by snarling people's sentinels.

Close by, from icy springs of great men's will,
An effervescent mountain torrent gushed
Through well-grazed fields of poetry and art,
Before it joined the city sewers, to be
Defiled by vulgar democratic thought.

42 Philosophical inspiration

We rested in the bracken, admiring
The grasshoppers, as the philosopher
Warned of the dangers of our beguilement
By the world, but he seemed more drawn than we
To the pleasures of rural peasant life.

In the magic village of his childhood,
He paid homage to the common people,
Bound by their shared blood to a fertile earth,
And, with those *volk,* he feared a fallenness,
Inspired by urban decadence and Jews.

For in the selfish city dwelt the Jew,
Employed no longer as professor of
Philosophy, or prized as woman friend,
But demonised as artful parasite,
Or scorned as racially defiling whore.

We listened to the homeless cuckoo call,
Disclosing itself in the undergrowth
Until, portentously, its signal ceased.
Fearful of the bird's delight in freedom,
The local craftsmen caged it in a clock.

When he learned later what had been done, the
Philosopher of Being never blushed.
Black smoke from his barbecue curled above
The forest, a reminder that, in life
And death, existence has no predicate.

---

[1] German for 'being there', the term used by Heidegger to describe human beings' particular mode of being-in-the-world through their relationships with surrounding objects and members of their community, including their tendency to become preoccupied with the here and now in such a way that they lose sight of their potential.

Strictly an interpretation

"The philosophers have only interpreted the world in various
ways; the point, however, is to change it."   Karl Marx
(1845), *Theses on Feuerbach*, XI.

ʊᏟᎶ

The comrades of those active years are dead,
Buried in the rubbish bin of
Unrequited history.
The cause was all,
But lost,

As the twentieth century came to
A capitalist conclusion,
With a gaseous pint
Of lager, not
Real ale.

Flea-bitten memories of old campaigns
Peel off, like yellow paper from
The walls of damp back rooms
In seedy pubs.
I see

Us perching there, uncomfortably, on
Bar stools, planning revolution,
Late on Wednesday evenings,
Not with bullets,
But via

The ballot box, yet to little effect.
Ron, with powerful specs, white-collar
Worker, intellectual,
Who beavered in
The lab,

Urged us to be scientific socialists.
We were materialists, of course,
But not as others thought:
Too ethical,
By far.

I picture Geoff, who talked of Red Bologna,
And who gave so generously,
As if performing a
Civic duty.
Then Fred,

Who taught us to stand Hegel on his head,
But, when Duffy was elected
A E U president,
It hit him hard.
He quit

To go fishing for all the time he'd left.
We sold our paper when we could,
Explaining fluently,
To sceptical
Listeners,

The great advantages of communism,
Namely, prosperity and peace,
Of which neither was truly
Evident,
At all.

But still, I hear big Clyde-side Jimmy quote:
"That man to man, the warld o'er, shall
Brothers be for a' that",
And *To a mouse,*
From Burns.

We were like adolescents, in search of
Unconditional affection,
Loving our class with such
Intensity,
We choked

On the passionate lump that stuck in our throats.
You can scarcely credit it now,
When you bask in personal
Prosperity,
So snug

In a warm room, toasting the millennium,
But we were serious enough,
As we bought the last round
And planned the next
Picket.

When we walked out into the frosty night,
The air became electrified
With the sizzling spirit
Of the workers,
Who leapt,

With bright banners, over the barricades,
To give their lives for the commune.
It was desperate, though,
As time went by,
To watch

Our comrades struggling to believe themselves,
Their same sad rhetoric pouring
Uselessly, like froth from
Beer taps into
Buckets.

I woke with Hegel upright on my knee,
Concluding that I'd made no mark
Upon a scene, that all
My life, I'd worked
To change.

Committed to that topsy-turvy goal,
It broke my comrades' will to know
They'd spent their time only
Interpreting
The world.

Community (tribute to Nietzsche)

"Morality is the herd instinct in the individual."
Friedrich Nietzsche (1882), *The Gay Science*.

ॐ)ल्ऽ

The community's annoyed, they tell me.
It's up in arms, demanding this and that.
Invisible giant! I see only
Pale people, peeping from behind curtains,
At the unemptied bins of cynicism.

Community! The corner shop is closed
When local youths kick in the window front
To drunken shouts of 'Paki bastard out'.
Deprived of unofficial meeting place,
Community does not apologise.

Community is not a crowd, they claim.
It doesn't rise on millipedal feet,
Like the spectators at a football match,
To roar defiance at the referee,
Before police eject its writhing limbs.

For them, community is intimate:
A pensioner invited round for tea;
And quite unlike the people on the tube,
Crammed close like couples in the act of love,
While holding bodies rigidly apart.

Community's the mysterious glue
That binds us close together, they insist.
They make it sound like lumps of chewing gum
Stuck after use beneath the seats in bars,
Then transferred freely to the trouser leg.

Community's the worse for wear, they say,
Indeed, so drunk on protocol, it swears,
With commonsensical absurdities,
At passers-by, who choose to jettison
The junk of mores, modes and marriages.

I know that their community is dead,
Stabbed to the heart and buried near the shed
By disrespectful individuals,
While neighbours go on mowing weed-free lawns
Beneath the shade of tall Leylandii.

It's rumoured that community's reborn
As ghost to haunt suburbia! They say
That it's indecently revealed itself
To worried ladies walking dogs in parks,
Who fail to honour poop-scoop etiquette.

Now god is dead, they cry 'community',
Believing it will come again as flesh
To quell the fear of burglary at home.
In spite of all the action taken in its name,
It's never even paid a doctor's call.

Community's a perfect fantasist!
Ah, Nietzsche, you would recognise the face!
Beneath its false moustache, it masquerades
As caring love, while exploitation forms
The real quintessence of communal life.

Paradise lost

"Two of far nobler shape erect and tall,
Godlike erect, with native honour clad,
In native majesty, seem'd lords of all,
And worthy seem'd: for in their looks divine
The image of their glorious Maker shone…"
John Milton (1667), *Paradise Lost.*

ഇരുഇ

In pursuit of ambitious objectives,
Our charismatic creator shaves off
The hoary beard by which he's recognised
To become a benign eugenicist.

He aims to improve on his earlier
Work which evolved, quite by chance, without help,
From the primeval porridge he'd left to
Decay and bubble away in sunlight.

This middle-aged Caucasian, in white
Lab coat, experiments with human life,
Magnifying the flawed double helix
To eliminate its imperfections.

Initially, he tolerated faults
But has become fastidious of late,
Excluding all but in-vitro methods
To achieve a sterile environment.

He is no longer prepared to allow
Haemophilia, or original sin,
Cystic fibrosis, or diabetes,
And other hereditary conditions.

Gyrating the juice of chromosomes,
He proceeds to construct a new order
For humanity of intelligent,
Vigorous and attractive specimens.

Unlike the mutants that preceded them,
With ape-like posture, feeble minds and
Ridiculous aggression, these beings
Are meant to show amazing improvement.

Verily, they are the children of God,
Meticulously procreated in
The lab by an omnipotent father
In his very own image and likeness.

Official propaganda leaves no room
To doubt that those, with genes thus modified,
Come well equipped to vault the crescent moon
And claim their place among the Pleiades.

Meanwhile, on Eden's lush green playing fields,
The new Caucasians, young, gifted, white
And sparkling with the promise of their birth,
Are tutored in the rites of leadership.

With the genetic code unscrambled, they're
Made flesh, to dwell among the common folk,
Though they still talk about our errant genes
To justify why we're confined to earth.

Respected for the virtues that they bring,
They drive in triumph through Jerusalem.
Acutely conscious of their genius,
We line the streets, saluting with our palms.

We're far too deferential and polite.
'Have a nice day', 'enjoy your meal', we shout
And yet, however hard we try to please,
These perfect creatures turn their heads aside.

Proximity has bred contempt: they note
Disease, stupidity and ugliness.
With other deities, they hate our faults,
But will not help with a redemption plan.

Brave world, be sure they won't reserve a place
For us at their exclusive restaurant.
If infinite in their perfection, then
How could they treat us with such arrogance?

CARIBBEAN THEMES

Mother-in-law thanksgiving

In 1998, Caribbean communities throughout the country celebrated the fiftieth anniversary of the voyage of the Empire Windrush from the Caribbean to Tilbury dock in London. The discharge of the ship's 500 passengers on the 22 June 1948 was seen as marking the start of post-war Caribbean migration to the United Kingdom.

Invited to attend and speak at a local Windrush celebration, I composed the following poem in honour of my intrepid mother-in-law, who came to settle in the West Midlands in those post-war years, when housing was in short supply and racial discrimination rife. The poem was well received both by the audience and by Epsi, herself, the kindest and most generous mother-in-law you could ever hope to have.

ജീഔ

Formerly of Jamaica, now
Resident, Birmingham, England.
Address: 1 Clent Villas, red brick
Victorian terraced dwelling
Opening onto a car-choked street
On a gloom-grey December day.

Big Ben chimes as we ring: Epsi,
Mother-in-law, plump in doorway,
Beaming a welcome: hot, hot, hot.
Wondrously bold in printed frock,
Grey plaits peeping from old straw hat.

"Nyam-nyam[1] will full you belly but
Breeze can't full you" Thaw out di bwoy[2]
With glowing heart, gas fire and soup.
Guileless goodness, unrefined kindness,
Tasty relish like chocho[3] and
Coco[4] in thick red-pea pottage.

Relaxing royally with Red Stripe[5]
Beneath the queen's portrait, we draw
The brocaded curtains, shutting
Out damp unforgiving England.

We talk about the promised land:
St John's red hills[6] and limestone crags
Where Epsi's roots grew strong among
Yam vines and ackee trees[7]. In thought,
We see tatoo[8] and Spanish jar[9].
We visit papi's grave grown high
With ginger fire[10] and Joseph coats[11].

A pause for primal memories,
Disturbed by a slow awareness
Of the ticking clock (the jewel of
Epsi's parlour). Respect acknowledged,
Our tale resumes, as Epsi rides
With jack fruit[12], duppy[13] too, on sad
Donkey down to Linstead[14] market.

Epsi, you warm and tasty like
A buttered breadfruit, roast on stove.

Epsi leaves for Spanish town[15],
Has pickney[16], keeps a stall and saves.
Then on to Birmingham to work
As seamstress at a hospital,
Using her homely handicraft
To mend the nurses' uniforms.

Retired now, she works for Jesus
By polishing the house of prayer.
Bless you, Epsi, your spirit is
As light as a hibiscus flower
Peering up to receive the Lord.

Integrity in Babylon[17]
On a gloom-grey December day.

[1] 'nyam-nyam' is a patois term meaning food, meal or eating.

[2] 'di bwoy', patois for 'the boy'.

[3] Chocho is the green fruit of the climbing vine, Sechium edule, eaten as a vegetable.

[4] Coco is an edible tuber or rhizome.

[5] Red Stripe is a Jamaican larger beer brewed by Desnoes and Geddes, Kingston, Jamaica.

[6] St John's Red Hills are mountains in the Jamaican parish of St Catherine.

[7] Ackee trees (Blighia Sapida) bear a fruit which provides a cream-coloured food.

[8] A tatoo is a small house or hut, originally with a thatched roof.

[9] A Spanish jar is an earthenware urn used for storing water.

[10] Ginger fire or fire ginger (Alpinia purpurata) is a plant with spikey crimson bracts.

[11] Joseph coats (Codiaeum or Euphorbia), sometimes called crotons, are shrubs with variegated leaves, like Joseph's coat of many colours.

[12] A jack fruit is a large football-like fruit which grows on the trunk of the Jaca tree (Artocarpus integrifolia).

[13] A duppy is a ghost, or spirit of the dead, said to accompany the jack fruit to market.

[14] Linstead, renown for its market, is a small town in the parish of St Catherine.

[15] Spanish Town is the parish town of St Catherine, and former capital of Jamaica.

[16] 'pickney', patois for 'children'.

[17] 'Babylon' is a biblical allusion to the home of non-believers, hence England, and a punishing life among white people.

The milk of human kindness

Beneath the creaking coco palm,
Granville's old mother, almost blind,
Seated on a three-legged stool,
Dictated a wishful letter
To her only son in England:
"Aunt want lickle money fi food,
Fi buy new Sunday frock, fi mend
Di zinc roof wha leak in di rain."

On reading the letter, Granville
Imagined his mother, vigorous
And young, head wrapped against the sun,
Standing before their wooden house
On blood-red ground. He'd played games at
Her feet, while the seed coconut,
Then buried with his navel string[1],
Took root and grew towards the sky!

Granville, who'd worked hard all his life
Without a break, a glazier
By day and a door man by night,
Decided, after twenty years,
To fly home for a holiday.
With conscience stirred by time away,
He took eight thousand pounds in cash
To buy some comfort for his mam.

His frail old mammy bawled with joy
When Granville came along the path
To stand beneath the coco palm
That towered above her little house.
A cousin clambered up the tree
And, with a sharp machete, chopped
Down nuts to greet the prodigal
With sparkling juice and tender flesh.

While friends and family sat around,
He told them of ambitious plans
To buy his mammy Sunday clothes
And build a bigger, concrete house.
That night, three men with guns broke in
By climbing up the coco palm.
Though he explained his mission there,
They made him give them all his cash.

Then with a gun against his head,
They forced him to his mother's bed
And blew his brains out with a bang.
The milk of human kindness spilled
As if a falling coconut
Had smashed to pieces on the yard.
Convulsed with laughter at their prank,
The gunmen spared his mother's life.

When Granville's mam, in faded dress,
Had sung *the bells of heaven* hymn,
His cousins, wearing crisp new shirts,
Filled up the hole with blood-red earth.
On Granville's grave, a palm tree grows,
Weighed down by golden coconuts
Which give a curd so soft and kind
It heals the psychopathic mind.

---

[1] In Jamaican folk lore, a child's umbilical cord is buried in the ground and a young tree is planted over the spot. The tree becomes the property of the child and is called her/his 'navel string tree'.

OFFICE WORLD

Computer secrets

You, with the dark eyes smiling
Above the word processor,
Cheeks, dimples and lips hidden
By an electric blue screen,
Murmur your instruction in
Sweet microsoft syllables
To the curious learner,
Bemused by the fly-cursor
Fluttering at his window.

Only throw open the file
To your disciplined soul and
Let my pet mouse play freely,
Under fat Ganesha's feet[1]!
With my tense fingers resting
On the keys to deep secrets,
I need to interrogate
The silicon between your
Reason and my emotion.

As our thoughts, like Shiva[2], dance
In the great circle of light,
I shall type you a poem
On my bionic desire
(Exposing a part of me)
In smartly printed Roman,
Rippling from a white casket,
Or by electronic mail
To your private terminal.

My exhibitionism finds
No favour, I can see, from
Your enigmatic glance and
Effortless dexterity.
The ice queen of cyberspace
Keeps her feelings on a disk.
It's a very private place
Like the grave, running no risk
Of personal encounter.

Let the reality of
Our intimacy be spun
In a virtual web of silk,
On which we both, as spiders,
Might cavort, suck blood and mate,
Or on seeing each other
As spiders in a machine,
Be repulsed, at any rate,
Switching off what might have been.

---

[1] Ganesha is the elephant-headed Hindu deity of good luck and learning, often shown attended by a rat (or mouse).
[2] Shiva is the Hindu god of destruction and regeneration who, as Nataraja, is portrayed dancing in a circle of flame.

Computer Secrets was first published in Noor, NS (1997), *Candles in the Storm, an anthology of Panjabi poems,* Progressive Writers' Association (GB).

Technophilia

In apparent acts of necromancy,
Manicured operators gently caress
Computer skulls, like head-hunters' trophies
Impaled on iron poles about the office,
And provoke the proto-brains, encased within,
To act auspiciously in tribal matters.

Owen, who's wildly enthusiastic
In his appreciation of machines
That respond to obsessive attention,
Much as teacher to obedient child,
Sits with the box, gazing intently through
Its window, on an automorphic soul.

Communing, Faust-like, with pure reason,
He thinks the processed data will improve
The rumblings of an organisation
Whose instinctive values, surgically
Removed, have been replaced with mission, goals
And targets, measured systematically.

Perhaps his propensity for order
Is congenital, or did a fussy
Mother superintend the toy cupboard,
Keeping jack-in-the-box on the top shelf?
His enthusiasm shows that he's only
Just converted to a new religion.

Zealous catechiser of the new creed
Termed informatic reconstructionism,
He tries, with missionary force, to spread
The word to neophobic pagan people
Who resist the intrusion, defending
Their paper citadels like angry wasps.

Owen dreams in cerebral silicon,
Of perfecting his administrative
Super-systems, algorithmically
Purposeful and logically intact.
The native people in the market place
Are more preoccupied with food and clothes.

Apocalyptic, Owen, on his stallion, rides
With telematic nomads 'cross the world-
In-parallel, to paradise: the new
Cyberia, where lesser humming disks
Are perched in harmony in Babbage trees,
And dos graze near the jets and daisy wheels.

Cross legged in meditation, now disturbed,
Here sits the great designer, imagining
The universe in perfect steady state:
A cloying cybernetic harmony,
Disrupted only by the philistines
Who gouge out chips with a vengeful loathing.

Quality control

By five o'clock, the contact lens is sore
Against the retina, the face it taut
And final fax is terser. The cerebral
Tasks, engaged in by the work force,
Are like spider's bites: they ingest the brain,
And leave the twitching body tenderised.

The clattering coffee cups arrive like
Car components, just-in-time.
The staff who serve the opiate insist
They're not impersonal automata
But a rebellious band of players
Unfettered by a predetermined script.

In daily intercourse across the floor,
Job titles are exchanged for first-name terms
And the sugar of weekend gossip stirred.
Then slowly, body shapes are recognised
Heaving like well-set jelly in scabbards
Of stiff blue-suited uniformity.

Between the key boards and the telephones,
Professionalism - that much-buttressed rock -
Attempts to stem the sultry lava flow
Of daily passion, meandering past
Striated rules, to congeal as basalt
On plains of ministrative compromise.

Colleagues have rearranged their diaries, cleared
Their cluttered desks and finally found time
To divest the hidden assets of the firm.
Collaboration through memoranda
Finds sudden explosive fulfilment on
The rough pile of industrial carpet.

Paper clips unbend, and the beetle, trapped
In the crystal paper-weight upon the desk,
Tenses inside its glassy tomb until
Its prison shatters in a thousand pieces.
Unperturbed, it crawls off to copulate
Under the mesmerised gaze of management.

Soft, among the desiccated files,
The human warmth of common enterprise
Surmounts with stealth the bureaucratic goal,
Transforming personnel to sentient folk,
Who live at work and, through their vibrant bonds,
Make systems that move mountains and themselves.

Lesson in leadership

He lounged
At a big desk
As chief executive
Issuing outrageous orders
To his faithful staff, of whom I was one.

In times
Gone by, I heard
Him cogently affirm
Commitment to a common cause,
And thought that he could make a difference.

I saw
That turbo thrust
Of purpose in his deeds,
At first, a seed upon the path
And then, a tree uplifting paving slabs.

I came,
Too slowly, though,
To realise his deeds
Were not assuaging social need,
But fed a boundless appetite for power.

Perhaps
That's why he shunned
The sound advice of friends
And chose instead the company
Of sycophants, whose praise and sly remarks

Provoked,
Pathetically,
Like wicked Iago,
His ridiculous jealousy:
A superman, afraid of others' worth.

He sucked,
Nonchalantly,
On a cigarette butt,
Obscuring my vision with smoke,
Always so certain in his conclusions.

Too late,
He'd lost the strength
Of my profound respect:
His megalomania destroyed
Democracy and reasonable debate.

He taught
Me lessons in
The art of leadership,
Confirming loyalty (as well
As love) must always be conditional.

I could
Never again
Allow myself to be
Persuaded by his rhetoric,
As it kicked out, like a hot-tempered horse,

Against
The flimsy fence
Of my troubled logic,
Impaired, as always, by a deep
Appreciation of his achievements.

Easy
To dismiss me
As traitor but, had I
Gone before his integrity
Was drowned, like a fly, in a whisky glass

Of mad
Self-indulgence,
The moral edifice
Might not have crashed so readily
Into a gaping sewer of cynicism,

And then
The consequence
For all who followed him
Would not have been so serious:
Respect and dignity just stripped away.

His part
I can excuse.
But my complicity
Was unforgivable: I did
As he asked, when I thought it ill-advised,

No, wrong,
To do his dirt
On trusted colleagues who
Had worked so hard for worthy aims:
I wished that I'd refused him there and then.

Too late
For leadership
From me. Not only did
I take the same direction as
Mein Führer, but I let myself be led.

Sex pest in the office
(Quasimodo and Esmeralda)

Quasimodo of Notre Dame,
Though twisted in frame, was upright
With virtue. Our hunchback, likewise,
Applies himself with laudable
Dedication to his labour
In the cathedral of commerce.

His ugly proportions were not
Apparent at birth but have grown,
With recurrent stooping, to fit
The green leather chair in which,
Like a frog, he's crouched for long years
Behind larger and larger desks.

On the bleak mornings before work
As his waxen body soaks in
The warmth of his glass-fibre bath,
He sees himself as a candle
Melted and globulous, burned down
On the high altar of profit.

He reveals his inner feelings
When grimacing at the mirror
In the marbled lavatory.
His deep self-loathing is always
Disguised beneath a garish tie
And obsessive regard for sport.

Seated in the antechamber,
Esmeralda, dark and soft-eyed,
Completes her chores methodically.
As secretary, she's never
Typed personal letters for him
But she would, if he asked her to.

With bowed head, she smiles, knowingly,
But rarely unveils her secrets,
Preferring to impress her boss
And other suited admirers
With the quiet efficiency
Of a well-organised office.

The calmness of her temperament
Caresses the casualties of
Frenzied work-place travail like the
Prayers of a contemplative nun,
Confined to a comfortless cell,
Amid medieval turbulence.

Waited on with such devotion,
The hunchback loosens his braces
And leans back, counting his blessings
On plastic rosary beads of
Routine reports and hot tea served
With a dutiful politeness.

Behold a modern miracle:
He levitates above his chair
When Esmeralda, drawing close,
Dispels his desolate nature,
Like a ray of morning sunshine
Streaming through a lancet window.

He whispers to himself her name:
"Dear Esmeralda, gipsy queen."
He yearns to tell her how he feels
Yet hastily averts his gaze
As, inadvertently, she leans
Across the photocopier.

Dry and resinous as old wood,
His exterior manner hides,
Like a carved misericord,
An underworld of fantasy
Unbefitting a celibate
Or devoted professional.

Impounded in a cage of love,
He wants to be her dancing bear
Led by the nose at her command.
He'll caper round the cabinets
While, on her thigh, she'll tap to time,
A tea tray as a tambourine.

At work, he's dragged a heavy cross
Towards a distant calvary,
But hopes that, on his journey there,
She'll wipe away his sweat to find
The image of his blemished face
Impressed upon her handkerchief.

His gentle unrequited love
Appears as a white dove, with rose
In beak, fluttering before him
Up flights of endless spiral steps.
Breathless, he tries to catch it, but
It vanishes into the sky.

She senses his affection now
For, when she gives him work to sign,
His pent-up feelings shake the pen.
Sufficiently discomforted,
The gypsy queen successfully
Applies to work for someone else.

"You have been sweet to me" she says,
"But I've acquired another post".
He longs to hide a note in her
Sandwich box, urging her to stay,
But fire bells in his head have warned
Him of the likely consequence.

His fantasies unabated,
The hunchback now pictures himself
In a violent Autumn gale,
Like a gargoyle on rotten stone,
Falling from the roof, still clutching
Her letter of resignation.

Perturbed by the melodrama,
His imagination slinks back,
Like a loyal dog, badly hurt,
Seeking safety behind the desk.
Scorched on the embers of love,
He howls with a harrowing pain.

Mixed verse: redundancy in the urban forest

In the urban forest, when the oaks died
The squirrels rummaged in vain for acorns
To hide among the broken bricks and glass.

Redundancies: she guessed they would occur,
For the irrefutable logic of
The balance sheet led inevitably
To staffing cuts by natural wastage
And then, from volunteering at a price,
To the swift dismissal of the work force.

Discoloured leaves fell from the ailing trees
To lie in rotten piles upon the tarmac paths,
Hiding the sticky excrement of dogs.

Despite knowledge, experience and skill
Beyond accountants' facile measurement,
She lost her job and came to doubt her worth.

However frequently they walked that route,
The passers-by eschewed each other's glance
And seldom ever asked the time of day.

She came to understand herself in terms
Of those she'd never met or spoken to,
Who had no concept of the work she'd done.

One evening, for a laugh, some youngsters tossed
The picnic benches in the pond and snapped
The newly-planted sapling trunks in half.

Naively, she believed that managers
Applied criteria objectively
To pick their staff for fiscal sacrifice.

A hissing swan ensnared by nylon thread
Was so distressed that its aggression checked
The brave attempts to rescue it from death.

Yet her self-evident intelligence
Made nonsense of the managers' pretence
To base their work on firm reality.

Screened by the trees, a woman begged a man,
To sound of blows, to stop him beating her,
While he, unmoved, roared loud obscenities.

Unlike the schemers, aiming for the top,
She took the mission to her heart, but then,
Her clear reluctance to reduce her staff,
The help she gave them in their fight for jobs,
Destroyed her record for efficiency
And led to reassessment of her work.

The urban forest hid a vicious gang
Who mugged the local folk at fearful cost
To principle, prosperity and pride.

TOWNSCAPE

Castaway

This poem was inspired by the homeless old man, reputedly of Eastern European origin, who lived for many years in a tent pitched on the central reservation between the busy lanes of the Wolverhampton ring road. Tolerated by the authorities, he became a living landmark to passing commuters, queuing in the rush hour traffic.

ঝেউগ্র

To my good eye, I hold a telescope,
And am surprised to see a man, like me,
Inhabiting an island cut off from
The city by a wide tarmac ocean.

A bearded castaway, clad in oilskin,
Like a captain, has pitched his tattered tent
Near bushes on the narrow strip of land
Between the north and southbound carriageways.

Lashed safely to my motor, cruising down
The road, I look across the traffic lane
And spy him foraging for stranded sprats,
(Old butt ends jettisoned by motorists).

A shell-shocked victim of an ancient war,
When faith and hope were swept away and drowned,
He hides himself in wreckage of the mind,
Impassable to prying bureaucrats.

Like actors' make-up, sediments of grime,
Discharged on him from numerous exhausts,
Have brought new colour to his character
And camouflaged his ugly inner scars.

Except for rats that gnaw the garbage sacks,
And nervous pigeons strutting on the verge,
He's cut off by the ebb and flow of cars,
And lives alone in roaring solitude.

In spite of flower beds, this is barren ground,
Well strewn with pages from the tabloid news,
And bottled messages for help, thrown out
By suicidal travellers in queues.

As yam and coconut cannot be grown,
The food is smuggled in by passers-by
Who hope for guidance from the bearded sage
On emigration to the promised land.

As if intoning a thanksgiving prayer,
His jaws engage in ceaseless exercise.
He scratches rhythmically as evening falls,
His figure haloed by the neon lights.

This, surely, is the paradise we crave,
Scratching our heads, perhaps, beneath the palms?
Although the breakers bathe the body clean,
They don't delouse an irritated soul.

Wrapped like a sailor in a fog of dreams,
He trembles, staring into space beyond
The office blocks, imagining, it seems,
A galleon ploughing through the murky haze.

I, too, have searched for ships that bore a freight
Of freedom's limpid pearls: and I, like him,
Have yearned to steer my destiny alone,
No longer moored by social anchor chains.

Ave Maria

In a deserted street, she stands alone
With arms akimbo, a dark silhouette,
Clasping the silver cross around her neck.
The moon is a neon sign and the star
A blue beacon attached to a white car.

Maria, ever virgin, always waves
Derisively as the police drive by.
They stare intently at her minute dress,
That rides up her buttocks and plump belly,
To display the calves of her long black legs.

Tonight, her breathing grips the frosted air,
Like well-trodden tyres on a screaming bend.
Suddenly, her pretty face, ugly with
Cruel experience, contorts in pain,
As sharp as a kick in a tender place.

Abandoning her pitch, she staggers to
A bar, warm with the smell of fags and beer,
To plead for help, but Joseph, pimping, smooth
In a camel hair coat and broad-rimmed hat,
Demands his cash and bundles her back out.

What, no room at the inn for sentiment?
While the angels croon an obscene chorus,
She turns to the dangerous night, forcing
Herself, now water-wet, along dismal
Alleys, to a place of assignation.

There, as a stray dog pisses up the wall,
All by herself, on a disused car seat,
Panting like a punter, amid torn rubber,
Maria gives birth to her Christ child,
Storing him with care in a cardboard box.

Touched by the sight of this nativity,
One man gives money unconditionally,
Another rolls a spliff of frankincense,
While the duke of dominoes buys nappies
And a supply of antiseptic cream.

Soon afterwards, alerted by a spy,
Herod's social workers smash down the door
And seize the infant, carrying him off
To institutional captivity,
Leaving the pitiful mother distraught.

We pray now for the holy family,
Since trashed, begot by an unknown father,
Delivered by a mum of little grace,
And long forgotten by a Christmas child
Who keeps a silver cross around his neck.

Easter resurrection

A restless night spent at Gethsemane,
Before he became resolute.
Leaving his wife in pain upon the bed,
He opened the front door to stare,
Finally, at their beautiful garden.
After the showers, a bright Easter
Had dressed her favourite lilac in pearls!
Since winter time, the lawn had grown
Increasingly more difficult to mow.
He took the hose-pipe from the shed
And made his way to where the car was parked,
Polished and shining on the drive.
Then, to the exhaust, he hitched the hose-line,
Threading it through wisteria
Into the bedroom via the window frame.
The blackbird sang, the air was fresh,
Before he jammed the accelerator
Pedal to the ground and retired
Under the rose arch and into the house,
To the roar of the car engine.
The day before, the social worker came
To tell him that, unless he had
A hoist installed, all care would be withdrawn.
A note was left upon the bed.
Once more, he studied his beloved wife,
Incontinent from Alzheimer's,
Declining to the point of no return.
Each held a lily and they kissed,
Then lay together and lost consciousness,
Drawing the curtain on their lives.
A friendly neighbour heard the car and came
Across their twin-bed crucifix.
She moved the stone slab where they kept the key,
And opened up the catacomb.
They both recovered in the hospital,
A resurrection miracle!
The neighbours brought them chocolate Easter eggs

And bouquets wrapped in cellophane.
But she was transferred to a nursing home
Where, with yet more floral tributes,
She passed away just one month afterwards.
When he was discharged from the ward,
Police indicted him for the attempt
To murder her. He readily
Confessed. He wished to die for her, he said,
To save her further suffering.
He mows the lawn and polishes the car,
(A puzzled judge threw out his case).
Though firmly resurrected in the flesh,
He spurns the news of Pentecost.

On cue

We flock with spectacles and walking sticks,
In faded clothes from forty years ago,
To squeeze submissively into the slots
Of time a welfare state must allocate
To stop life ebbing from us while we queue.

At eye infirmary reception desk,
The poster promises us patients care
And courtesy, in circumstances that
Respect our privacy and dignity:
The dignity of waiting in the queue.

The room is full of older citizens
Who come, with life-time partner or alone,
To sit subdued and still on pale brown chairs
In silent rows, until the nurses call,
Unless, through sleep, we miss our place in queue.

Our human worth is starkly measured in
The value of our time: the old endure
The passive purgatory of wasted hours,
While doctors have their minutes supervised.
For lives spent waiting, we in queues accuse.

The illusory affair
(forever Valentine)

On St Valentine's day, she takes
Delivery of a large bouquet.
She resolutely fills a vase,
Destroys the heart-shaped greeting card,
Crumples the cellophane, and hides
All traces in the pedal bin.

Late at night, he has answered the
Telephone to silent listening.
Once, at the lights, he imagined
He saw her car with passenger
Seat occupied, but concluded
He'd mistaken the vehicle.

The whispering to women friends,
The pattern of her overtime,
And her cold shoulder, turned in bed,
Are hidden by a hologram
Of normal domesticity,
Which he refuses to question.

To items on their credit card account,
His eyes are strangely blind,
Withholding from his conscious mind
The startling charges from boutiques
That sell silk shirts and ties (though he's
Received no presents, recently).

When driving now, he seldom plays
Music on the car radio
And averts his gaze from bill boards
At news vendors, which glamorise
The careless fornication of
Television celebrities.

His concerned companions, better
Informed by the smoke of rumour
Than by any conspicuous
Fire from wifely indiscretion,
Daringly suggest that he find
Solace in flesh-pot fantasies.

Believing, somehow, he's to blame,
He thinks about their gap in age.
Forcing his stooping shoulders back,
He seeks visual reassurance
Of his bodily proportions
From every reflective surface.

On supermarket shopping trips,
He buys more single instant meals,
Loading the trolley with canned beer
And bottles of own-brand whisky,
For cheap solitary drinking.
She stays away for longer now.

He tries to reassure himself,
With an album of photographs,
That his years of married life are
As satisfactory as the
Happy-ever-after endings
He's read about in magazines.

Confessing to an affair, she
Informs him that it's over and
That she wants to stay. Hearing with
Deaf ears, he simply won't accept
She's been remiss in any way,
Insisting she's his Valentine.

I am the motorbike

Dedicated to my friend, Paul Willis, who first introduced me to the esoteric sub-cultural meanings of the motorbike, this poem alludes to the Hell's Angels Motorcycle Club, founded in 1948 by bike-riding US servicemen, who, it is claimed, took the name from the nose-cone art of a B17 bomber. The Angels did not admit black people or women to their chapters and practised horrific initiation rites. The verses that follow describe my more introspective personal feelings about bikers and biking.

ॐ

I am the motorbike,
No longer merely flesh and blood,
But with tattooed wrists tapering
Into cattle-horn handle bars,
Inseparable prostheses of
A mind, moving so fast, it lives
Only for the moment!

I am the angry bull,
Pawing the ground with screaming tyres,
Hot blood and fearsome bellowing,
Impatient for the sacrifice.
Then, with a judder, thrown forward
On the asphalt plain, with my heart
Pumping adrenalin.

I am the bullet man,
Dipping hard into a fast bend:
Heaven's curling meteorite,
Wind stinging on my radiant cheeks,
Blowing me backward at a speed
At which I glimpse the death's-head moon
Floating, with me, through space.

I am the cyborg king,
Part humankind and part machine,
Enthroned above a petrol tank
And throbbing with the will to power,
Destined to rule necropolis
With scorpions and robot arms
In grease-stained leather gear.

I am the nose cone of
A bomber plane that drops its load
On route to pandemonium.
When ant-sized people see me fly
With chrome-tipped weapons on my wings,
They hold their ears to stop the noise,
Then run away to hide.

I am the angel damned
To burn up everlasting hell,
Pledged always to defy the god
Who dominates the corporate world.
I pass his limo on my bike,
Then turn defiantly to wave
My piston in his face.

I am the master race
Of masculine, two-wheeled machines,
Destined to power across the wastes
To lynch and rape the lesser breeds,
Until what's soft and warm in me,
The yellow stinking egg that's left,
Is dashed against a truck.

FRIENDS, FAMILY AND SELF

Bereavement in bright colours

This poem, which frightened family and friends, was written when I was made redundant after twenty years of full-time employment.

ೞಞ

Instead of their normal attire,
The sombre suits of the workplace
Worn for traditional farewells,
The mourners dressed in bright colours
To disguise the pain of their loss.

I attended the funeral
Of somebody I did not know
But, as the casket slid slowly
Towards its incineration,
I learned how others had seen him.

The wreaths bore messages, yet I
Noticed only the white daisies
In the garden of remembrance.
Later, a reception was held
At which old friends shared memories.

He'd been a successful salesman
And a chauffeur to famous people:
A happy and contented life,
It seemed. In conversation, I
Was questioned on the work I did.

If I'd said I was unemployed,
Without a job, they might have thought
I'd acquired a private income
Through financial speculation
And was concealing my status.

But, in truth, I was without work
And had lost my identity,
Almost as if I were the man
I did not know. Feeling ashamed,
I claimed that I was between jobs.

If the question is asked again,
I'll pretend to be a poet,
Dressed casually for bereavement,
Wreathing myself in white daisies
In remembrance of employment.

Breast cancer

Through your T-shirt, my eyes devoured your breasts,
Two pomegranates, brown, erect and firm.
When pins impaled the crimson seeds inside,
You thought I'd lost my appetite for you,
But what I craved was of a different kind,
Far more essential than a callused rind.

Frozen objects: an autobiography

I have frozen the objects of my life
Inside a set of crystal paperweights
Arranged in sequence on the mantelpiece.

That plastic globe, once blessed and brought from Lourdes,
Had pride of place within the family shrine.
With adults out of sight, we children shook
The souvenir and watched the dandruff snow
Rise up to cloud the waxy virgin's smile.
I tried at first to change the world by prayer,
Requesting action from a distant God,
But never grasped the logic of the scheme
To save the world by dying on a cross.

The metal, lodged within that ball of glass,
Was taken from a *lazy dog*, a bomb
Of razors used to rip away the flesh.
Stamped with a circle and inverted Y^1,
It sits as warning in my living room.
Fearing the shrivelled buds of spring would die
Along the hedgerows of my earnest heart,
I marched in hope, along a glistening road,
To stop the silver fire of final war
And, by my protest, bring the world to calm.

When miners went on strike, I bought that chunk
Of frosted quartz as contribution to
Their hardship fund. From caverns underground,
A man, begrimed with coal dust, shines his lamp
Into the granite face of government.
I yearned for peace but thought it could not come
Without the workers in grey overalls,
Their voices deep beneath a smoking sky,
Parading ever onwards, banners red,
To claim their just reward for sweat and toil.

I climbed a barren mountain to look down
Upon an Eden, full of flowers and fruit,
To where white Adam lived with his black Eve.
On my descent, I killed the racist calf
And sought to procreate Jerusalem.
For me, that vitreous whorl, condensing two
Pure streams of glass, one black, one white, in ever
Closer convolutions sets the scene:
The double helix of the mixed-race child
Demands from us a unitary theme.

Last of five objects is that resin skull
A death's head held, like Yorik's, in the palm,
Reminding me, not of mortality,
But of its former occupant, the brain,
In concert with its feral friend, the mind,
Which, as a teacher, I set out to free.
For everywhere, the intellect was boxed,
Tied up with custom, poverty and fear.
Through education, I believed we could
Uplift our lives in creativity,
And come to comprehend the universe.

Reminder of enthusiasms now gone,
Those objects of my life are moribund,
Like fetuses in clear formaldehyde,
Illustrative, but only to the point
Of termination. I regret nothing,
Not wasted effort, nor imprisonment
In the bubbles of my own invention,
But at my age, spare me any further
Millennial fantasies, for I want
Only those objects that are in motion,
Alive, like lustrous darting butterflies,
Not fixed and fossilised in amber glass.

---

[1] The symbol of the Campaign for Nuclear Disarmament.

Driving angrily to change the world

In your youth, when your mind was sharp
And body muscular and slim,
You leapt into your car and drove
Angrily at the unfair world,
Hoping to knock it flying when
It didn't jump out of your way.

How soon the view on either side
Would change if you sped fast enough
Towards the compelling image
Of the magnificent city,
Just visible at the end of
An intellectually straight road.

When the route to your dream turned out
To be more crooked than you thought,
You stopped at a service station
For coffee, career and family,
But, longing still for a new world,
You took again to the highway.

The traffic crawled at a snail's pace,
As drivers edged cautiously past
The spots where people lay trapped and
Mangled in the grim wreckage of
Institutional juggernauts,
Jack-knifed upon their human loads.

On seeing the casualties,
Travellers imagined awful
Possibilities for themselves,
And began to count their blessings,
Eyes fixed on the fender in front
And blind to bolder horizons.

As the evening gloom descended
You switched on powerful headlights, dipped
To avoid dazzling other folk.
Too late, the beams picked out a dog
Which ran in front, to be struck down,
Howling, before it could escape.

The car radio broadcast news
Of endless traffic jams ahead.
At the wheel, with your corpulent
Body belted firmly in place,
You recognised reluctantly
That you were caught in the slow lane.

In despair, you sounded the horn,
But soon came to regret the chorus
Of protest your blaring provoked.
You had set out to change the world
But all you'd been able to do
Was to stop it destroying you.

ITALY

Night in Assisi

Assisi is a medieval town built of pink stone on the slopes of Mount Subasio in the region of Umbria in Italy. It is the birthplace of Giovanni di Bernadone, later to be known as St Francis. Born in 1182 into a wealthy merchant's family, Francis chose to live a life of poverty, simplicity, chastity, obedience, and respect for his fellow creatures.

In Assisi, itself, is the thirteenth century Basilica of St Francis, built in three tiers on the steep hillside, with the tomb of the saint in the crypt, then the lower church and, above it, the upper church, each decorated with the most beautiful frescoes. In the upper church, Giotto's frescoes show scenes from Francis's life: for example, his vow of poverty, the sermon to the birds, the gift of the stigmata, and the occasion of his death.

This poem, however, was largely inspired by a late-night visit to the nearby sixteenth-century church of St Mary of the Angels which was constructed to contain and preserve the Porziuncola, the simple chapel in which St Francis is believed to have died. My lasting memory is of the overwhelming tranquillity of that scene.

ಬಆಚ

In Umbria, among the olive groves,
Our brother, Francis, lies at peace upon
The chapel's stony floor. His ashen face,
Lit only by the melancholy moon,
Still shows the smile with which he greeted death
As singing angels winged aloft his soul.

When young, he stripped and gave away his clothes,
Renouncing all his rich inheritance,
To preach the pleasures of the poor man's life.
His tunic, made of coarsest cloth, rides up
To show his callused feet incised by nails,
His gift from god for love of Jesus Christ.

The roses cast by fluttering doves create
A gentle rustling in the tranquil night.
Beloved poverty, his closest friend,
Supports his head upon her scrawny breast,
While, in the ring of shadows, beggars cower
And crouching wolves beseech with mellow eyes.

Although he knew the burdens born of wealth,
Our Francis was no proto-socialist.
In sympathy with Jesus crucified,
This blessed saint would practise chastisements,
And fast, and kiss with rapture lepers' sores,
Debasing flesh to purify the soul.

Eight centuries have passed since Francis lived,
But poverty, grown long in yellow tooth,
Survives in sordid hovels near the towns
And, far away, in sun-parched famine lands.
No longer wandering as a mendicant,
The old dame rides behind an army tank.

The virtue of renouncing wealth to lead
A simple life in service of the poor
Is still respected, even in our time,
But is gaunt poverty in such demand
That her sharp countenance can be preferred
In place of measures for her prompt dispatch?

If only Francis could have lived to see
The vast productive power of industry
With its miraculous ability
To eradicate hunger, cure sickness
And confine redundant poverty to
A frescoed vault below Subasio!

But poverty's death has not occurred:
The children's bloated bellies are the same
And eager crows come flocking round the dead.
The rich and powerful do not share their lives
With people tainted by the teaming slums
And the alms they give are of another kind.

In truth, we do not value human worth,
Nor choose to build god's kingdom here on earth.
Meanwhile, in absence of a better way,
The doves will carry roses to the poor,
And they'll embrace their sister poverty
In Umbria, among the olive groves.

Anita Garibaldi

Anita Garibaldi was the Brazilian wife of Guisseppe Garibaldi, the charismatic Italian revolutionary, who led the struggle for Italian unification and national independence, known as the Risorgimento. In 1848, during the great period of European revolutionary upheaval, Pope Pius IX, threatened by liberal forces, fled from Rome, where an independent republic was declared.

Guisseppe Garibaldi led a group of volunteer soldiers, later to be known as the red shirts, in defence of the new republic, and was joined on the battle front by his wife, Anita. When the French army under Marshal Oudinot arrived in 1849 to restore papal government, the red shirts bravely repulsed the French attack on the Janiculum Hill.

Rising steeply from the River Tiber, the Janiculum provides magnificent views over the city of Rome. Statues of Guisseppe and Anita have since been erected there, under the giant pine trees. Mario Rutelli's statue of Anita, on a horse, was presented by the Brazilian government in 1935, to honour her Brazilian origin.

In July 1849, refusing to accept defeat, Guisseppe and Anita, and all who were prepared to follow them out of Rome, crossed the Apennines, avoiding French and Austrian armies, until they reached the neutral Republic of San Marino where, surrounded on all fronts, they disbanded their followers. Guisseppe, accompanied by Anita, six months pregnant and already gravely ill, set out to reach Venice. In the district of Comacchio, near the Great Lagoon, Anita died in her husband's arms. Her body was concealed in a shallow grave. Those who participated in the uprising, or assisted the fugitives in any way, were brutally punished or executed.

In the year 2000, Pope John Paul II, ignoring protests, beatified Pius IX, the last pope king, putting him on the road to sainthood!

ଔଓ

Timeless, in sculpted form, high above Rome
On the Janiculum hill, brave Anita,
Garibaldi's wife, on a white charger,
Rushes to defend the young republic,
Her dark eyes glowering at its foes.

In morning sun, we tourists turn our backs
And snap the panoramic view below,
Until it's time to climb aboard the coach.
The ragged crows sit squawking in the pines,
Like priests in conclave at the Vatican.

Though big with baby stirring in her womb,
She left the children at his mother's house
And sped through hostile battle lines by night,
Just like a glowing meteor on course
For Garibaldi, Italy and Rome.

Her husband greeted her with tenderness,
But begged her to return at once to Nice.
When she refused, he introduced her to
His officers: "This woman is my wife:
One more fine soldier to support our cause".

And other women fought for freedom, too.
When French shells hit, young Pozzio, convulsed
With grief, embraced the broken body of
A friend. His puzzled comrades found it was
His wife, disguised in crimson uniform.

We wince at the inscription *Rome or death.*
So hard for us, relaxing here, to grasp
The readiness with which they gave their lives.
As black as soot, the pine trees form a cross
Against the brightness of the setting sun.

Despite a costly sacrifice of blood,
The red shirts could no longer hold the walls.
Refusing to surrender to the French,
Or watch the futile slaughter of his troops,
Bold Garibaldi offered them a choice.

"Your Rome will always be where your hearts beat.
If you should come with me, we'll carry Rome
With us, until we win it liberty,
But I can promise only hunger, thirst
And pain on ever-moving battle fronts."

Thus warned, and for a country not her own,
Anita joined the line that wound across
The barren hills, into a distant haze,
Pursued by hungry wind and enemies,
With scarecrow soldiers marching to their graves.

Remarking on the panoramic views
Of rock, ravine and river, far below,
We drive the same route on the motor road.
Aggressive regiments of sullen pine
Line up for combat on the mountainside.

In San Marino, she fell gravely ill,
Yet still refused its sanctuary,
Insisting she would journey on with him,
By land or sea, to Venice and beyond,
Until the whole of Italy was free.

With Austrian ships in close pursuit,
They beached their boat near red Comacchio,
Where Garibaldi waded through the surf,
Bearing Anita gently in his arms,
And sought a refuge near the Great Lagoon.

By banks of reeds beneath a wooded ridge,
He wheeled her fevered body on a cart,
Until they reached the Mandriole farm.
There, as their enemies grew near, she died,
Ordained for glory at her husband's side.

Protected by a parasol, we sit
In contemplation, gazing at the sea,
Then, with Frascati, toast her foolishness.
In the distance, shimmering in the heat,
A row of pine trees spikes the faded sky.

The corpse was hidden in a pile of sand,
With exposed limbs devoured by animals.
They knew her by the fetus found inside.
But still, Anita's damaged body wore
A crimson cloak, her Roman uniform.

Antonio Gramsci Avenue

Antonio Gramsci (1891-1937) was a founder and general secretary of the Italian Communist Party. After the fascists outlawed political dissent, he was arrested and imprisoned. Because of ill-health, he was released eleven years later, to die soon afterwards in hospital in Rome. Gramsci was a contemporary of Benito Mussolini, the Italian fascist leader, or duce (pronounced 'duchay').

As a prisoner, Gramsci filled thirty notebooks setting out his political and philosophical views. Emphasising the role of ideas, and the effectiveness of human effort in history, he developed the concept of hegemony to describe the way an exploitative bourgeoisie, through the exercise of moral and political leadership, establishes and maintains control, even in a democratic system in which workers and peasants are in a majority.

In Florence, an avenue has been named after Antonio Gramsci. While walking there, I saw a blind man accompanied by a guide dog.

ಬಾಂ಄ಬ

The sun-tanned Duce, bobbing and
Weaving in expectation of
Assassins' bullets, is driven
In triumph through Rome. A Caesar
In breeches cracks his leather will
Upon the crowds who yelp with joy.

Sallow-faced, beneath spectacles,
From his long incarceration
In a cramped and dimly-lit cell,
Antonio Gramsci, prisoner,
Declared subversive by the state,
Reflects on why we live like dogs.

Heedless of his own confinement
In a catacomb of concrete,
He is aware that, when chained to
The cosy kennels of tradition,
We do not snarl, but become charmed
By the poetry of angels.

He has had dreams of Sistine walls,
Seeing the Last Judgement in his
Revolution. That's why, for him,
The soaring superstructure of
Ideas swirls free and effortless
Above its economic base.

Yet frescoes of memory retain
The stark hierarchies of heaven
To which we aspire, for who cares
For a dog's life? Only beggars
Kneel before priests in gratitude
For the blessing of poverty.

And that's far-fetched for beggars, too!
So how do we explain that, in
Democracies, unmenaced by
The snarling fangs of fascist squads,
We gnaw at meatless promises
And growl as guard dogs for the rich?

Beyond the tarmac of the state
Are sprawled the dusty pathways of
The civil world, where routinely
We take our daily exercise,
Lingering, now and then, to sniff
The reeking fasces[1] of elites.

Habituated creatures, we,
Who lope the squalid alleys of
A savage market place in search
Of scraps and openings. With common
Sense, we could create our own
Magnificent hegemony.

Comrade, the social democrats
Subvert the message of your notes
And build corrupt alliances.
Master and loyal friend remain
Inseparable, and romp with
The Duce's children in the park.

In Florence, home of monuments,
Where city squares are scattered with
White crumbs of marble wedding cake,
A guide dog helps a blind man walk
Antonio Gramsci Avenue[2],
Made famous by a prisoner's name.

---

[1] Fasces: a bundle of rods with a projecting axe blade used originally as a
symbol of the Roman magistrates' authority, subsequently adopted by the Italian
Right-wing nationalist movement (1922-43) whose name derives from it.
'Fasces' sounds very like 'faeces' (waste matter).
[2] Viale Antonio Gramsci, Firenze.

WALES

Mermaid murdered at Llandanwg

Dedicated to St Tanwg, a fifth-century missionary from Ireland, who may have founded it, the church at Llandanwg in north central Wales is situated near the natural harbour created by the river Artro flowing into Cardigan Bay. Storm-blown sand dunes still threatened to bury the little grey church and its surrounding slate gravestones.

As a child, I imagined, mistakenly, that Llandanwg was the setting for Matthew Arnold's poem, *The Forsaken Merman*, but what follows is best understood with the plight of refugees and immigrants, rather than merfolk, in mind.

ജരുഗ്ജ

Some fifteen hundred years have passed
Since Tanwg came by coracle,
As stranger to a pagan land,
To build a chapel on the sand.
Paddling barefoot through the breakers,
He chose to preach to gulls and whales,
And blessed the merfolk with his staff
For their help in troubled waters.

Under dark translucent clouds,
A semi-human animal,
Mistaken sometimes for a seal,
And glistening like a silver coin,
Came hobbling from a choppy sea,
To cross the shingle shore, and duck
Beneath barbed wire, into the dunes
That overwhelmed an ancient church.

For many years, when spring tides flowed,
A mermaid visited that spot,
Where Tanwg landed long ago.
She'd creep beside a slate stone tomb,
Which showed, despite its weathering,
A sharply chiselled epitaph,
And place a wreath of seaweed there,
While murmuring a foreign prayer.

In the rain, I, too, had seen her,
Reclining on her fish's fin,
And staring sadly at the grave.
Serene she was, her flesh exposed:
Not pallid like an upturned cod,
But dark as night without the moon
Or stars, her woman's breasts as oiled
And even as an ocean calm.

The minister objected, though,
Not merely to her nakedness
(Provoking him to carnal thoughts),
But to the fact that in his view
The hybrid creature had no soul,
Yet trespassed in a sacred place.
He thought the alien should leave,
Despite her tendency to grieve.

Early twentieth century version

Egged on by biased parishioners,
Two farmers caught her by the tail,
And tied her in a hessian sack,
Then tossed her, squirming, in the brine.
When washed up later on the shore,
The bag was buried in the dunes,
Without a headstone, or a wreath,
And at a distance from the church.

Late twentieth century version

Swayed by indignant residents,
Two yachtsmen caught her by the tail,
And teased her as she writhed about.
As rape was not an option here,
They struck her with a piece of slate,
And left her body on the dunes,
Where ceaseless rain disguised her tears,
And all her sorrows decomposed.

Twenty-first century version

Two youngsters on a weekend break
Amused themselves at her expense.
As rape appeared impossible,
They masturbated on her scales,
And cut her with a razor blade.
They left her body on the dunes,
Where what was human decomposed,
While lashing rain destroyed the clues.

The scene is magical, indeed:
The church, the sky and wind-swept beach,
But when, to shelter from the storm,
A stranger, black and bowed with woe,
Appears with wonder in our midst,
Why disregard her simple needs,
And treat her with barbarity?
No fabulous illusion, this!

The road from Eisingrug
(climbing the Rhinog mountains, Gwynedd, North Wales)

From Eisingrug, I walk the narrow road
That wriggles like an eel around the hills
To reach a rolling pasture where, dispersed
As dandelion clocks, the sheep crop short
The shallow turf enclosed by dry-stone walls
Adorned in lichen torques of embossed bronze.

Between the dragon-warted crags, the track
Ascends towards the pool of Eiddew Bach:
A toad's eye, mingling animated bright
Reflections of the cloud-swept sky with
Shimmering reptiles, cold and aqueous.
While catching breath, I plumb its coiling depths,

Then, searching Zion, climb once more the foot-
Hills of the sky, grey Ysgyfarnogod,
The mount of hares, before the squalling rain-
Showers, needling on the flesh, enforce my shelter
In the entrance to a disused mine,
Whose lodes exude the fetor of decay.

With rain-drenched landscape wrapped in mist, a sudden
Gust reveals a planing precipice
To scree-strewn slopes and cwm below. A slate,
Dislodged, must skim an age before the echo
Of its clattering fall returns to taunt
The ear with danger's dread proximity.

The draught of solitude tears loose the mind's
Communal certainties, like tufts of moss,
To bare the greywacke of unanswered whys.
I see no pattern to the splintered rocks,
No purpose, save the one I choose to plant
With iron soles upon an unmarked track.

A gliding buzzard plunges to the sedge,
While, in the west, a ray of sunlight shafts
The scudding clouds to luminate
The mystic Isle of Saints. And, slow, the sea
Consumes the wafer sun, transforming all
To gold, before the black finality.

Harlech Point

We two
Remain apart
On a deserted beach,
Imprisoned by the sea and sky,
Which merge at an ambiguous margin,
Discarding their identities in soiled-sheet mist.

The storms,
That lash this coast,
Have littered rippled sand
With strange fragmented artefacts
From a prurient civilisation
Where sea gulls squabble over sanitary towels.

When joined,
Casually,
In shameless solitude,
Beneath an obscene, empty void,
Bereft of universal meaning, how
We thrash in vain for ever-absent inner joy.

I squeeze
Your breasts, their skin
Opaque as plastic sheets,
And stare, in horror, at your blank
Unyielding eyes, sulphate-of-copper blue,
But luminous, like squid, in ultra-violet light.

Obscure,
In the distance,
The invasive sea roars
Like traffic on the motor road,
Drowned out only by the piteous sound
Of white cars, shrieking to some dour catastrophe.

Barefoot,
We shudder at
The touch of seaweed fronds,
As lank as hair, shaved from the heads
Of victims manicured for holocaust,
Their corpses tossed in pits behind the marram grass.

The waves,
Which rise and fall,
Remove the feeble marks
That we impress upon the shore,
And ridicule our rapturous intent
With wanton, surging, masturbatory displays.

Despite
Our heaving lust,
The seas of reason ebb
And strand us on these shallow banks,
With all the junk from Noah's ship-wrecked ark,
To wait our fate beside the bones of guillemots.

About the author

Who's Frank Reeves? Who cares? Nobody, of course, except his immediate family, a few close friends and he, himself. Why would you want to know? You aren't required to decide on his suitability for work, or to make excuses to others for his conduct! And it's hard to imagine that he'll achieve notoriety or fame.

As this book's author, however, he's made his poems available to you. They're intended to exist on their own merit, with a life independent of him. Nevertheless, should you choose to read them, a little knowledge about his background, beliefs, preoccupations, and purposes, might help you to understand his idiosyncratic treatment of subject and theme. The bare-boned biodata are:

Location: born and brought up in Bournville, Birmingham; resident, for much of his life, in Wolverhampton, England. *Education*: university, with degrees in philosophy, education, sociology, and race relations. *Occupation*: works for Race Equality West Midlands. *Marital status*: married to a Jamaican, with three children of mixed race. *Belief systems*: existential humanist, socialist. *Political vision*: a peaceful, prosperous, democratic, racially-equal society. *Fears*: being alone, pain, blindness, paralysis, corporate capitalism, megalomaniacs, planetary despoliation. *Obsessions*: important, but private, personal matters. *Travel*: Europe, Asia, America, the Caribbean. *Favourite places*: Merridale, Wolverhampton; Ynys Llanfihangel, North Wales; Linstead, Jamaica; Greece; India; Italy; Morocco. *Literary genre*: urban counter-romantic. *Reason for publishing poetry*: persuaded, against his sceptical inclination, of its social and political potential by the great Panjabi poet, Niranjan Singh Noor, the enlightener, now deceased. *Address for correspondence:* 9, Oak Street, Merridale, Wolverhampton, WV3 0AE. *Telephone:* international 44 - 1902 - , national 01902 - , local 429166. *Email:* f.w.reeves@cableinet.co.uk.

Progressive Writers' Association (GB)

The Progressive Writers' Association (GB) was established in 1969 to promote and enhance the Panjabi language, literature and culture, in all the major cities of Great Britain.

The branches of the Association hold regular literary meetings. Major literary conferences are organised every two years in different parts of the country.

Between them, the Association's members have published over seventy books of poetry, short stories, novels, travelogues, literary criticism and philosophy.

In addition to promoting Panjabi language, literature and culture, the main objective of the Association has always been to promote racial harmony and fight injustice in whatever form it takes.

The Association has played an active role in encouraging the teaching in Great Britain of Panjabi from the most basic to postgraduate level.

If you require more information, please contact our general secretary, Darshan Singh Dhir, at 72 Crathorne Avenue, Wolverhampton, WV 10 6 BU.

Education Now

EDUCATION NOW thinks that the word *education* has come to be misunderstood. Many people assume that it means 'what teachers do with children in school' and nothing else. **EDUCATION NOW** challenges that view. Its understanding of education is much wider, encompassing the many beneficial experiences which take place outside schools and colleges and which lead to valuable learning. It opposes those elements in the present system which promote uniformity, dependency, and often, a lasting sense of failure.

The vision of **EDUCATION NOW** includes:

- a focus on the uniqueness of individuals, of their learning experiences and of their many, and varied learning styles.
- support of education in human-scale settings including home-based education. small schools, mini-schools and schools-within-schools, flexischooling and flexi-colleges.
- recognition that learners themselves have the ability to make both rational and intuitive choices about their education.
- advocacy of co-operative and democratic organisation of places of learning.
- belief in the need to share national resources so that everyone has a real choice in education.
- acceptance of Einstein's proposal that imagination is more important than knowledge in our modern and constantly changing world.
- adoption of the Universal Declaration of Human Rights in general and the European Convention for the Protection of Human Rights and Fundamental Freedoms in particular.

EDUCATION NOW maintains that people learn best:

- when they are self-motivated.
- when they take responsibility for their own lives and learning.
- when they feel comfortable in their surroundings.
- when teachers and learners value, trust, respect and listen to each other.
- when education is seen as a life-long process.

EDUCATION NOW is a forum in which people with differing, diverse and undogmatic views can develop dialogue about alternatives to existing dominant and compulsory forms of education.

For further information and the latest details of publications from the **EDUCATION NOW** publishing co-operative, contact the office at the address below, or visit the website at:
http://www.gn.apc.org/educationnow/

Office: 113 Arundel Drive, Bramcote Hills, Nottingham NG9 3FQ

Index